"The beauty, intensity, and breadth of E. J. Koh's work continues to transcend to new levels. Her language is transformative, making history more alive than we can feel and understand alone. Here is a chorus of lives and a song of peace. With *The Liberators*, Koh cements her place as one of the greatest Korean American writers of our time."

—**JOSEPH HAN**,
author of *Nuclear Family*

"E. J. Koh brings a poet's eye and sensibility to this remarkable novel. Here you will find characters and sentences that will leave you gasping for more. *The Liberators* captures grief and paranoia and a legacy of colonialism and violence with beauty and measure and grace." —**MATTHEW SALESSES**,
author of *The Sense of Wonder*

"E. J. Koh's *The Liberators* is a sublime achievement for its deft political and emotional intelligence, its fine-tuned grasp of how a divided country divides lives through the generations. As in all great works of art, it uses the earthbound to transport us to a realm that feels like it's been unperceived until now. As readers, we enter a theater of raw perception. A tree falls out of nowhere, a boar walks into a room unannounced, shadows shatter across a ceiling. Illumination can happen at any turn, reminding us that there's always more world than we've had the capacity to see."

—**PAUL LISICKY**,
author of *Later: My Life at the Edge of the World*

"An elegiac, ferocious, and deeply stirring novel. E. J. Koh melds image and story together precisely, holding up to light the history and making of Korea. I loved *The Liberators* not only for what it shows us about our world, but moreso, ourselves." —**CRYSTAL HANA KIM,** author of *If You Leave Me*

"*The Liberators* is a poetic breath, the language as haunting and epic as its story of a divided country's legacy and impact on the Korean diaspora. I'll read anything that E. J. Koh writes." —**KRYS LEE,** author of *How I Became a North Korean*

"As readers of E. J. Koh's *The Liberators* we're asked to occupy the boundaries of a divided country, the world of two colonizers, and a family's eventual journey to America where the demarcation lines shift to the palm of one's hand, in the heart and life lines, where the words for love and survival are spelled out in the hand, where Koh's lyrical narrative hand is held over our hearts in undying allegiance." —**SHAWN WONG,** author of *American Knees*

"E. J. Koh's poetic voice lends itself beautifully to the aching slowness of the search for healing. This book is about intergenerational trauma but it is also a celebration of intergenerational hope. Koh tackles history and sorrow with a delicate hand." —**ROWAN HISAYO BUCHANAN,** author of *The Sleep Watcher*

"E. J. Koh brings her elegant poet's hand to this intimate and expansive mythic novel of four generations of a family suffering sudden absences and war, seeking love and connection, weighted with the complexities of no easy answers. I didn't want this book to end." **—JIMIN HAN,**
author of *The Apology*

"A piercing, patient debut by one of our finest chroniclers of American han. You won't know what hit you until the final, perfect image." **—ED PARK,**
author of *Same Bed Different Dreams*

THE
LIBERATORS

ALSO BY E. J. KOH

MEMOIR
The Magical Language of Others

POETRY
A Lesser Love

THE
LIBERATORS

A NOVEL

E. J. KOH

TIN HOUSE / PORTLAND, OREGON

First US Edition 2023
Printed in the United States of America

Manufacturing by Lake Book Manufacturing
Interior design by Beth Steidle

Library of Congress Cataloging-in-Publication Data

Names: Koh, EJ, 1988– author.
Title: The liberators : a novel / E. J. Koh.
Description: First US edition. | Portland, Oregon : Tin House, 2023.
Identifiers: LCCN 2023025051 | ISBN 9781959030157 (hardcover) |
ISBN 9781959030225 (ebook)
Subjects: LCGFT: Novels.
Classification: LCC PS3611.O3659 L53 2023 | DDC 813/.6—dc23/eng/20230613
LC record available at https://lccn.loc.gov/2023025051

Tin House
2617 NW Thurman Street, Portland, OR 97210
www.tinhouse.com

DISTRIBUTED BY W. W. NORTON & COMPANY

1 2 3 4 5 6 7 8 9 0

For borders—real and imaginary

CONTENTS

THE
LIBERATORS

I

INVISIBLE LINES

1980–1983

I

YOHAN

Daejeon, 1980

BY AN EARLY AGE, I COULD READ AND WRITE IN SIX languages. I found a tool—an ink brush, a twig, or my stub finger—and used it to draw a character on parchment, dirt, or air. When one line touched another, my heart reached my fingertips to impart meaning. At five, it was for pleasure that I left words all over town: on a tree, I carved *tree*; in the river, I spelled *river* in pebbles; on my mother's dress, I inked *dress*. At some point, my mother set me down and didn't pick me up again. On my mother's grave, I wrote *grave*. I was just a boy at the end of Japanese colonial rule. I wrote my words as if I couldn't live without them, as if I were made of nothing but words. I classed *rock, plant, animal, man,* and *God.* I observed a patch of weeds and then myself in the mirror to see the differences between *plant* and *man.* Between them was a middle point, or *animal.* I asked what stood between *man* and *God,* but the grave said nothing. I watched the country divided up as spoils of war. When I was fifteen, I was taken in for vandalism and sent to the military. I labeled my boots *boots,* and my gun *gun.* I spelled *fire* with sticks, lit it up in flames. Penned *grenade,* pulled the ring. My last words I wrote on the side of an ICU tent, filled with my dismembered comrades, in the blood I owed them: *death, death, death.*

After my years in the military, I was made of silence. I carried out my duties quickly and without protest. Peeled out the bunks, torn and stiff, and myself, thirsty and whiskered, I worked the sprawl, search, and rescue; leashed the dogs; unspooled rope; baked bodies; collected resin for fuel tanks; plunged drills down holes; poked at slugs with my rifle. One day the older recruits marched me to the showers and told me to get prim. I accepted two medals for protecting foreign dignitaries. My director and department were shocked to hear I wanted to retire to a lowly auditor at the age of twenty-four. They were puzzled by my decision, but after a roomful of handshakes, after I'd surrendered my clothes for the next soldier, my leaky and clouded binoculars, and a tin of hand-rolled cigarettes, I was installed in Daejeon as the youngest superior at the office. I so assumed my position nobody called me again.

I never asked what wonders I might have been capable of had I been left as the boy filled with words, or whether foreign dignitaries might have come from across the ocean to witness how I read and wrote throughout fall, winter, spring, and summer. I pictured my mother outside my room, telling visitors not to wake me since I needed my rest, and myself, stirring up with a smile before I snuggled back into the covers. I didn't regret that she had died before the surrender since she had not lived to see the war. Rather than words—using them whenever it snowed or rained or blossomed or the sun touched me on my way to the office—I grew skilled in courting. It didn't come easy, but I understood courting fundamentally. Courting was forcing a thing to become unlike itself. I had become removed from my own nature. So I married and had a daughter. I changed the structure of myself—an animal into a man—to love my wife. Then only life could change what God intended to be human into an animal, even into a plant, vulnerable to the crush of a heel or an aneurysm. To replace a rock in the ground with my wife, then my wife with a gravestone on the surface.

~

ONE MORNING IN 1980, I was in my midforties, when I picked up the phone and called my employee. At twenty-three, my daughter was one of few unmatched girls her age, and my employee had two sons who wanted to build airplanes. His sons sketched planes on their napkins. A perfect tea set of aeronautical engineers. I rang from the guest room on the first floor, my late wife's room. The windows overlooked the steps to the entrance where tall iron gates jostled in the wind. The fog drew rosefinches, like blooms in the low bush, whose cries I mistook for rainfall. On the news, threats loomed—they argued about the North Korean underground tunnels. The third tunnel had been found some years earlier, less than thirty miles from the capital. Tunnels ignited fears about spies hiding among us. GIs left their bases and camptown brothels, in such numbers since the war, and arrived with the trains' pipe-organ whistles.

My employee answered with a smile in his voice. He said my daughter was a beauty, but she was the spitting image of her mother, who'd died from heartbreak. I said it was an aneurysm—he suspected it was the same thing. I was certain he meant no harm. My employee said it was natural that I wanted my daughter married, so I could bring another woman into the home. I would need a girlfriend soon. By the time I recognized his meaning, enough time had passed to make my silence inappropriate. I thought carefully of what to say: "A widower feels a widow's sorrow." My employee agreed that it must be lonely living with my daughter. He encouraged me to do what was in my best interest, like the Americans. I bargained for his youngest son. My employee said his wife wouldn't agree to it. She thought it too early for me to marry again. He'd rather talk about the riots and the spies from the North. After the phone call, I was discouraged enough to give up. But my late wife, Namjo, had told me it could be one man who turned our lives around, and wasn't that man also looking for us?

My daughter's room was empty. On the dining table, rice and soup bowls, two pale moons left under the lacework of a cover sewn by my late wife. I dug through my phone book, finding the matchmaker's number. She'd have no qualms because this was her business. But she, too, answered with a gripe. She said there should be a line of suitors out the door, but everyone was paranoid. Without peace in this country, what could we do but find peace in our homes? People would forgive me about my wife, but I better move out of the house because my son-in-law couldn't go into the kitchen without goosebumps. "A house with a heartbroken woman," she said, "can never be a home." That afternoon, I felt unwell and boiled water for tea. Why couldn't they invite us over for dinner and pull me aside and say I'd raised a good family? The problems with my choices could wait, but Namjo had asked me to secure a better home for our daughter. The drawers hid their knives. The drain filled with hair. Shadows of lilac stems crossed the room, so polite they could shut the door behind them. The floor pulsed with dust caught in the broad light. Namjo had always worn green, her ribbons like curling leaf tips—it brought me such memories. Then a sharp whistle on the stove.

CURFEW WAS TWO HOURS PAST. I switched on the television for the noise. It wasn't enough to drown out the voice of my late wife.

How can Insuk show her face to her classmates and teachers?

I didn't know, so I raised the volume. The news was censored. Nothing but a statement about a civil commotion. The protesters looked about Insuk's age.

We all grew up in one house and died in one house. That's normal. You can't buy a new house every time somebody croaks.

I thought my wife would've liked a new house away from everyone. On the television, I spotted my employee's youngest son, his school ID hung around his neck.

They talk like that because I'm dead. Yohan, when you're dead, they won't remember the awful things they said to you.

The student protesters had been lined up.

Why're they scaring those poor kids?

Namjo kept her carriage upright no matter how restless she felt, her hands running along the side seams of her dress.

They look like Insuk, don't they?

The brigade raised their rifles. I recognized the slight movement before the stillness of their aim.

Yohan.

Their stance was so rigid you could've picked them up and their bodies would have remained in their exact position. Their skin and uniforms I could tell reeked of smoke. The light that reflected on their helmets also reflected on their boots. Their fingers relaxed in the crooks of the triggers, all their weight and strength gathered in their jaws with no expressions on their faces. Their eyes dilated as they emptied their cartridges of bullets into the students.

Yohan!

Among them, my employee's youngest would leave no record of his arrest and death, and no meaning at all.

Yohan, go!

Perhaps he realized this truth as he looked toward the sky and shook as if his body were a garment on a clothesline.

~

I PACED THE MAIN road for an hour. I had my head on backward, eyeing passersby. After the coup d'état, martial law was enforced and spread like ink on wet paper, bleeding university closures and mass arrests. They classified protests to end martial law as riots instigated by spies. The Korean military began a suppression campaign to win the country back, beginning in the southeastern city of Gwangju—the center of the protests—and the military was backed by American diplomacy flexing its muscles to practice war games. Aircraft were deployed. Tear gas was shot into buses, police batons waited at the doors. Truck beds with amps, empty wig shops, bodies on handcarts. We joined the twentieth-century tradition of killing Koreans, as if to say no one can do it like us.

Now of all times, I recalled that the bookcase once fell on our baby daughter. I'd gone to stop it, but the hefty books crashed down, and my wife threw herself on top of our daughter. I never thought to do what she did—it was the difference between us. Perhaps we ought to join my wife in the habit of the ground. There would be nothing for us to say once we had her to put all things into their place. She would tell us what had been set into motion—like a single thread unraveling a silk tapestry—when we'd turned against ourselves and called each other the enemy. What we had to forsake to lose a part of ourselves. The way a man could kill his own brother if it saved him from hating himself another second. I wanted to ask Namjo whether a country split in half was still a country. Perhaps it was more terrifying if there were no spies. If there was no one but us.

~

OUT OF THE DAMP mesh of night, I waited for Insuk in a nearby bar. It was L-shaped with one wall lined with lockers for college students. The tree growing over the building had thick branches, showing the bar's age. I took a seat at the window facing the one-way road going uphill toward my house.

A young man carrying books under his arm walked in. I recognized the books because my daughter had them. He was in the same year as her.

The young man was long and slender like a stalk of bamboo. His family must've been worse off. Few people would notice since he dressed neatly and looked at ease—a properly raised child—but I saw faint creases at the tops of his leather shoes. They were at least two sizes too big.

He sat at the window, one seat away from me.

As I suspected, he didn't order a drink. He grabbed a fistful of free macaroni popcorn. The owner complained it was for regulars and gave it to him on a napkin.

My attention drifted from my beer to the young man. He was bound to notice I was looking at him.

He kept his eyes on the road. "Can I help you, sir?"

"No, no, son." The young man could change into a looming figure in a short time if he willed himself to—the sort of man who had only brothers. I sensed a taut line of control running through him. Though it was clear he didn't want to talk, I couldn't help myself. "You're waiting for a girl. With the country falling apart."

"Just a friend." The young man was still staring ahead. "With all due respect, the country is falling apart because of people like you." It was an accusation.

"So it is a girl." I watched him for another moment, then said, "Your friend coming down that road?"

The young man looked at me and back at the road.

I was now certain he was waiting for my daughter. My house was at the end of that road. But the young man didn't seem to be aware I was my daughter's father.

"You're not at the protests," I said.

The young man tried to hide his agitation by feeling the bones in his hands. "The police will have their murders. The locals will have their graves." He put his feet on the ledge under the bar, winding his words up. "The state will have their memorials—erase our memories with national history."

"You aren't worried about the tunnels?"

"The tunnels are a ploy to make us feel contaminated with spies. It makes any action justifiable, as long as we can make ourselves clean."

"And where does your friend fit into your plans?"

The young man appeared to let his guard slip. "You can't tell her what to do." So he was in love with her.

Up close, the young man was dumber than I'd thought. Only his posture gave the impression of composure. "You're about that age. You done with your military service?"

"No. I have buddies who left already."

"Oh, your buddies putting down the protests on TV?"

"They're waiting for orders to retreat."

"I spent some years taking off my combat boots." I stole a macaroni, popped it into my mouth. "Problem is she won't wait for you to be done with your service. Happens to everybody. You're sent in, and the older guys who're done, they come back the same year as your girl, except she calls him oppah now. It's better to date after you're released. Someone younger won't resent you for leaving her so long, and she might like your stories."

During training, on the obstacle course, I couldn't fit into a narrow tube with the drinking of my college years.

As punishment, I'd had to clean the warehouse urinal troughs with a toothbrush. Still, it was easier than digging trenches—instead of a shovel, they'd given me a spoon.

"I got rid of all the spoons in my house. Nobody can use a spoon. Only chopsticks. We drink our broth by lifting our bowls to our mouths."

"What about your toothbrushes?"

I grinned. "Here, take my drink."

He declined and followed my gaze to the road. A soft light fell from the foliage above us.

"She's a little older than me. She took some time off because her mother passed." The young man was inquisitive. "Did yours wait for you?"

The question caught me unprepared.

"She did but only because she's so stubborn." I leaned forward with my glass. "My wife always said—if you have no teeth, then use your gums. But if my wife had no gums, she'd used her jaw bones," and we laughed at the picture.

The young man wrote on his napkin. Then passed it to me, saying he had written it down because it'd be rude to say out loud to his senior. I stared at the dark lines. "Your handwriting," and I touched the ink. "The hanja looks different."

The young man apologized. "I taught myself, so it looks upside down sometimes. But it's all there," he said. "The Chinese is precise. But the Korean is undeniable."

His handwriting reminded me of characters I hadn't thought of in ages, and I couldn't keep myself from tracing over the lines—crossing over to the boy at the river who had spelled with pebbles, who recognized the shape of his mother in the clouds, an angel I thought my mind wouldn't notice again.

On the napkin were characters for *good* and *man*.

Before I could answer him, my daughter appeared on the road in front of the window. The threat of curfew couldn't disrupt her slow and even pace. She stopped before us.

It was the young man's turn to show his shock.

He looked at my daughter and me with newfound recognition. The young man now seemed to take hold of the reins he had let go of earlier while sitting with a stranger. He greeted me for the first time and bowed from the waist.

~

BACK AT MY HOUSE, the young man apologized again for not knowing who I was. Normally, I took the sofa, but I sat on a floor cushion across from my daughter. The young man kneeled on a cushion by the door.

"You can't live by yourself," I said to Insuk.

Her eyes lit up like rooms. "I can't leave you, especially right now."

With my wife gone, Insuk released the knife of judgment I held against my own throat. But her consideration of me made me sorrier. It was fair for my daughter to despise me—the gates were still slick with her tears, their dark footprints over the stone steps. Her mother's black-ribboned photograph greeted her under the stairs.

"We will find you a husband." These next words were meant for the young man. "I've set up a few blind dates for you, Insuk."

She pointed at the young man, whose face went red.

I felt as if my daughter had come to my aid. "Who exactly is he to you?"

"He would do anything for me."

"I'm sorry about all this," said the young man.

"Good," I said to her. "He has kind eyes."

Insuk kneeled and forced the young man to move closer. His shirt was drenched in sweat.

"We're going to get married," Insuk said.

"Sir, I don't know what to say."

"Only if you agree to it," I said to her.

Insuk nodded. "Then we can do it tonight."

"Tonight—as in get married?" he asked.

I turned to Insuk. "Are you sure?"

"I'll get our nice glasses and the oak-aged soju in the pantry." She fetched the soju and the glasses and filled them.

We each took one and raised it. Insuk proposed that we finish the bottle that night. It was this sense of celebration that had drawn me to her mother.

"What's your name, son?"

"Sungho," she said slowly. "Sung-ho."

The textured walls looked soft like napkins. The cushion's peony pattern. My hand, blooming capillaries. I noticed for the first time, under the stairs, Namjo's small smile—it was a privilege, the conversation between a man and his late wife. "Sungho," I said to him. "Even lifting a sheet of paper is better done together." I understood the urge to dig a tunnel and go underground and live in the perpetual dark. Like a children's game where hiding was equally motivated by the desire to be found. To pass through a tunnel was to one day be seen. To be a spy was to one day be known. Even the dead, in the grips of dying, were as close as possible to feeling alive.

2

SUNGHO

Daejeon, 1980

SUNGHO KNEW INSUK HAD NO CONTACT WITH men other than her father. She told Sungho in their first year of college that she thought you became pregnant if you sat in a chair a man had occupied a second before. The heat left behind was lewd. Her mother had warned her to be cautious of touch's shadow. Insuk kept her utensils separate and hauled her bags herself, changed pants after school and avoided shaking hands with men outside her family. There was no sitting unless it was on the ground. To touch somebody through an object or sense the body's warmth was to share one's intangible essence with another person. A touch could touch you everywhere. Still, there was no doubting her libidinous nature when she confessed she thought of him at night. No denying the pleasure she must've felt in dodging him for years. Followed by the thrill of their arms brushing as they walked along the river.

Now arranged to be married in their fourth year, Insuk sprawled on the same riverbank at Sungho's feet. The stony light turned everything gray. His fingers settled in the grass.

Insuk asked him to join the protests. "We have to do something."

How quickly her reserve was forgotten in a time of military rule and dictators, a time of kidnappings and torture. At twenty-three, Sungho found himself a nihilist about country but practical about love. Insuk wanted to join the nationwide marches. She showed him a flyer with an illustration of a hand reaching up out of the page. Sungho told her the man who printed it was dead before he hit the ICU floor.

"You're wasting your energy, Insuk. This poor bastard will never draw another picture again. You're a number in a ledger—for both sides."

Her attention went across the bridge. "If they arrest me, they can put me in women's housing. I'll finally have a suitable place to live."

"Don't make jokes. More like fabricate charges, same as what they've done to the factory girls. Open your coffin so your father can identify you, and then charge him for the wood."

"Why don't you want to join?"

"Insuk, please."

"Can you believe that poll? After the surrender, half the country preferred the Japanese to the Americans."

"How did you expect people would feel about the US military government?" Sungho no longer trusted talk of national independence. "We've got American employers now. Marching for democracy? It was the same with the Japanese. Nothing will happen until a good number of bodies are in the ground—until public services become quiet because they can't play the national anthem if you were murdered by the national police."

"You know all this better than me. You should be out there."

"Since my family's poor?"

"No. Because you're smart as hell."

Sungho let his lips almost touch her ear and said it took no skill to be smart. The slight noise she made when he grazed her reminded Sungho that he still looked for her feelings.

Sungho said, "I know my parents hated the Japanese so long, they started to hate the need to hate them. Your hate changes you. You hate them now because you want all your hate back. Because even your hate isn't yours anymore."

"Sounds like you prefer the Americans."

Grinning, he tossed a rock into the water. Despite the changing currents, the riverbed stayed the same. He told her time must pass for the river bottom to change in even small ways.

"Anyway," he said, "I have no choice but to live."

She gave no sign of listening, so he went on. "I've never had samgyeopsal before in my life."

Insuk stared at him. "You can't die without trying pork belly."

Sungho smiled, feeling her attention return to him. "See? No choice."

"I'm taking you out for your birthday."

"It's in May, a couple of days."

Her hands flew to her mouth. "You're younger than me," she said. "You have to call me noona."

"We'll be married," he mumbled, "and it won't matter anymore."

"How embarrassing for you," she said. "I'm April."

"You only have a month on me?"

"You're old-fashioned. You know one month is a lifetime."

The wingless cicadas slept in the grass. Insuk smelled of sweet fruit Sungho could peel slowly over hours. Soon he wouldn't be a stranger to her. He would be her closest ally and ahead of her own father. There would be a shared taste among their cups and bowls. Their books would share their fingerprints. Had she been thinking of Sungho when she asked about the protests? Sungho had no intention of letting her go when dead bodies barely legal enough to see the movies were lined up on their backs in government buildings and hospitals. "Sungho-ya," she said, "your noona's going to buy you samgyeopsal." Yet as the country stood on loose ground and prepared its giant leap, Sungho felt at home.

~

AT DARK, they made love as the river pulsed beside them. From next to his ear, she sighed—a sigh different from any either of them had heard before, like the way flowers sighed in the fields, nodding, ushering the wind and the leaves. The feeling shifted, and it was natural to pull her toward him, place his hands on her throat, his thumb resting on the bud of her lower lip, keeping it there until her mouth opened. Then another thrill as he laid fingerprints on her face and chest, holding her in one brilliant moment fluorescing into another under clouds combed like rabbit fur, and the wild eyes she had of an animal, her wet and warm breath, her palms roving lightly, like the wings of a bird, up and down his torso. Sungho squeezed his eyes shut, overwhelmed, and he tightened his grip and pushed her under him. He yanked her jeans down and her bare skin rose to meet him. To make love was to sink into the only river where you did not drown. They helped the blades of grass come to patterns of rest beneath their bodies in the night.

~

THE NEXT EVENING, Sungho waited by the river. The rocks underwater left a black smudge across the surface. Insuk was supposed to treat Sungho to samgyeopsal barbecue in the alley on his birthday. Sungho had refused at first because he wanted to pay but couldn't until he graduated and found a job. She'd told him not to fuss over money—how could he not go to a protest, or a barbecue? His reasons fell like a splash in the water, and Sungho didn't want to argue, so he'd said they might as well go.

Sungho waited at the bar down the hill until closing.

He stayed past curfew. He went to her house, but the lights were off.

Come morning, he was up early—in his sleep the library had come to mind.

The library was empty.

Sungho sat in front of her gates. If she didn't appear tonight, he'd take the bus outside of town to search for her.

Passersby knew that for no other reason than waiting could a man like Sungho be sitting by the two-story brick home with stone steps from the wrought industrial gates to the pitch of the double doors. Inside, a Western-style dining table. Chairs eighteen inches high—the same distance from your ass to feet as your head to heart. Round toilets like in the movies. Leather sofas and cushions. Celadon vases on glass shelves. One bedroom had the square footage of his basement rental. Sungho had no recollection of what he'd said to her father at the bar, and he feared it might turn out that for his daughter's sake her father had changed his mind about Sungho after all.

After midnight, Insuk came up the road.

She was in the light garment of her pajamas and wobbled on her foot. Sungho saw that it pained her to walk.

"My God." Sungho brought her into the house.

He placed her on the sofa and sat on the floor. Her father wouldn't have let him take the sofa while she was in the house.

Inspecting her feet, he found no broken bones. But there was a gash on her left foot. It was exposed and stinking. He pressed a cloth on it. "How did you get this?"

"It's my father. He never came home."

Sungho washed the gash out. "You're the same as him, reckless. Now's not the time to get hurt. Hospitals won't take you."

"He always comes home."

Sungho tried to contain his relief at her safe return. "Insuk, who knows? He could be on a work trip. He might've been delayed."

"He's not—he'd tell me."

"Maybe he headed south? You've got a shed full of jars in the back. He might've wanted to fill them before the markets close."

"No one's seen him."

Some might suspect her father if he didn't return. These were desperate times. They might say he needed money. Everybody was paranoid. You had to check every stone block on a bridge you crossed. "These days people disappear for no reason."

"What does that mean?"

He let his eyes fall to her foot. "Whatever he's doing, it doesn't look good."

Insuk said she could feel that her father was close by.

Sungho brought a basin of water, ointment, and bandages from the kitchen. He crouched to treat her. "You should've come to me first, Insuk."

Terrible things happened to people for no reason. You could be perfectly fine in the light of morning, and by the call of the moon, you could be lying in a crate packed soft with your body.

"I know you," and Insuk got up from the sofa. "You don't care about anybody, Sungho."

Sungho was struck for the first time by the expression on her face, as if by an arrow released from a bow. Her gaze was innocent, but no doubt he could read a threat there. She said things to Sungho she hadn't before. It could be as they feared, and they had come to realize, that the freshness and lightness of their relationship could fade in a moment. If they found her father dead, it'd be terrible for Sungho to be the one who was alive. It would be as if he'd killed her father himself. "I'll go find him," Sungho said. "When we come back, let's go eat something delicious," and then her eyes returned to their crescent shapes.

~

SUNGHO WAS ELEVEN WHEN his father stole him away.

Sungho remembered March 1968 as his father Jeha's work boots crossing the footpath and his oar-like arms carrying them over the fields. Sungho revisited that day to feel the weight of his father's memory, like a roof during the rainy season when the cracks would no longer hold.

They walked for two miles out of Daejeon.

For the next three, his father put him on his shoulders.

Sungho was a boy captivated by his feet floating above the ground. The grass as tall as his parents. Shadows of his fingers above him pointed back home. Sungho was lighter than he'd ever been, sitting on his father's shoulders. Sungho watched the freeways and deserts, pastures and railroads. He mirrored his father's quiet disposition, seeing the view from his perspective. His father was thirty-three.

At twilight, they met the last crosstie on the railroad track.

There, at the bottom of the hill, was a round of buildings.

His father pointed at a squat building apart from the others.

The building was painted orange across its facade. Coming down the hill, you could tell by the roof deck it'd once been green. Broken windows, filled with shrubs.

His father set him down outside the building.

"This is my favorite thing in the world." His father touched the exterior.

The building stumps had the sheen of white bone.

Sungho showed his disappointment. "It's only two stories." On the building sites where his father picked up jobs, Sungho had seen more impressive structures.

"I can hear it calling to me. We had a past life together. Maybe I was a building like this one." Where Sungho saw stone blocks, his father saw a system at war with gravity.

Sungho could appreciate modesty up to a degree. "How old is it?" Dried leaves sank into the building's rich gray loom.

"It was built before I was born. See the way the hill tilts over there with the newer buildings? Those buildings are meant to go up quickly and come down just as fast. They don't build them like this anymore. This building is the last of its kind."

Sungho asked what the building had been used for.

"All sorts of things. Hosted travelers. It was full of music and dancers. Once it was a place for people to pray. Now it's for people who remember it's here."

Sungho touched the broken glass.

"The top of the building is weak. There was a lot of weight on the top floor. So the windows were the first to go. The windows are the eyes of the building."

Sungho told him that buildings didn't have eyes.

His father asked if Sungho was sure he himself had eyes. You could see in many ways, and the most important seeing was done without your eyes.

His father talked to things. To sense the full weight of them, he kept a lightness in his body like a spring. "When the building is gone," his father said, "will you be sad?"

Sungho tried not to show his surprise. "Why would I be?"

"If you are," and he palmed Sungho's chest, "go in there."

He pushed his father's hand away. "Go where?"

"You have a place inside."

"I don't."

"How do you know?"

"Of course. I would know better than anyone."

"How about I give you this building?"

Sungho said, "I don't understand you sometimes."

"Close your eyes."

"Okay."

"Put your arms out."

"Okay."

"Pick up the building."

"Okay."

"Now shove it inside your chest."

Sungho pounded his fists and squirmed.

"Look at me," his father said. "Do you feel different?"

Sungho said he felt taller.

"If anything goes wrong, you can go to this place."

His father built a fire, but whether it had been raining, Sungho couldn't remember. Whether they'd chewed on squid or shoestrings, whether his father appeared brighter before the flames, whether their bodies left imprints in the dirt, whether the wind dragged them beyond the tracks and fields, back into the density of their lives, tight under the chin, and whether his father's laughter held some concern for what was to come.

They returned to their basement rental the next day.

Sungho ran to his mother in the metal doorway.

She caught him in midair like a pollock in her skirt.

Sungho's shirt was atop his head, his pants knotted around his torso, and he had on just underwear. "We swam across the river."

"You went as far as the river?" she said.

"Two rivers. Then we came to the end of the tracks."

His father stood behind him, radiant. "You're scaring your mother."

When she told Sungho to go inside, he refused.

"You go in," his father said to him.

Sungho went into the kitchen, but waited behind the door.

He watched as his father approached his mother. It appeared as if his parents would embrace, but they stopped short.

"He's the only one you couldn't leave," his mother said.

"I brought him back," his father said.

"Of course. You can't take care of him."

Sungho crouched into the doorjamb.

"You always do this, Jeha. You leave." Her face was pale like leftover rice water. "This time, we don't want you back. You don't have a place to come back to."

His father closed the door in front of Sungho.

When the door opened again, his mother walked past Sungho and his father didn't look at him. From where Sungho stood in the kitchen, he saw his father climb the north-facing slope of the main road. At the top, his father turned and waved to let him know he was going somewhere Sungho shouldn't follow. His father had a long stride and a narrow back. His shadow swung behind him like a shawl that folded him deeper into the road until he vanished into a thin line. On the first night of summer, Sungho would return to that building by himself, and when he reached the rooftop, he would lie down on the concrete to begin a new season of his life without his father.

AT DAWN, before anyone was awake, Sungho went to the police station to file a missing person report but hesitated because it was suspicious to go missing during the protests. The military associated an absence past curfew with commie activity. If her father couldn't be counted on to be at home, then maybe he was out organizing riots or aiding guerillas in the mountains. Sungho entered the station and filed the report anyway. Insuk's father had last been seen in a pale blue shirt. He had the sort of hair done at the salon—short sides, handsome like a clean head of cabbage.

The plainclothes officers at the station slouched with the same tightly rolled shoulders. All wore different-colored flared pants. They suggested that Sungho post a reward.

"The man's probably a fisherman," the first officer, in green pants, said to him.

"But the water's right there," the second one, in purple, replied.

"No, you idiot. He's out fishing for girls."

"Oh, I want to go fishing."

The red one bellowed, "Using what pole?"

Sungho held his breath. "Sir—"

"Then maybe we should try the gambling room. They're always open," the red one said. "Like your mom's legs," and the officers hooted.

The green one said to Sungho, "Try the ICU."

"No one's too fancy for an ICU bed," the red one said.

"Don't worry," the purple one said to Sungho. "He's probably safe. Americans are lazy, and Koreans are hard to kill these days."

Leaving the station, Sungho had no answers. Nobody bothered to explain themselves or say where they were going. It wasn't uncommon that the more Sungho could not get answers, the more he looked in outrageous places, like the buildings or the landscape, all of which had become circumspect. The hills had a gaze of their own. Columns of smoke. Mourners joined the protests. Many were the parents and grandparents of a femur in the soot. They stood upon a branch of war no one remembered in the forest of a much bigger war. Sungho felt something strike him in the back of the head, and he broke into a run for Insuk's house. No one was certain of the ideas battling for their innermost morals. It was darkest underneath the candlelight. They couldn't get away fast enough with their lives. Sungho closed his eyes as if he were shutting an iron gate.

3

GUARD

Daejeon Prison, 1980

VERDI'S "SEMPRE LIBERA," TRANSLATED AS "ALWAYS Free," played in the main cell, but only Guard understood Italian. He mouthed, *Follie, gioir*—Madness, euphoria. Head of the prison under the dictatorship at twenty-one and superior to guards twice his age, he was known by no other name than Guard. He stood by his afternoon prisoner, strung up by the feet. Guard fixed the prisoner's socks because the night was colder than anyone had expected. He was reading a report instructing on how to identify commies, sent over by the Americans at the central station. Looking at the description, Guard let his knife slip across the prisoner's throat, the final step of a careful process. Blood lassoed out of the body like wine. He washed at the tap behind the prison and saw another guard dragging a man in his fifties wearing a pale blue shirt. The man fit the description of a commie in daylight: *An overzealous liberal professor . . . tweed jacket . . . closeted homosexuals . . . anybody who studied abroad or travels often . . . a person of noble birth . . . experts on China . . . educated foreigners.*

The man, by appearance, qualified as a commie, or at least as someone who harbored pro–North Korean sentiments. The man spoke in fluent English to the GIs. He could be part of a labor union, controlled by North Korean spies who infiltrated their meetings, or he could be a Korean American, one of the permanent residents of the US who were deported by their country to the South on suspicions of sympathy. These things came with a harsh penalty. Those who worked under Guard's command feared his knowledge of torture. Guard could imagine himself as the prisoner, and as the knife cutting into the prisoner, as the hand holding the knife, and as the silence along the path of the knife. This man, like the others, would be executed. GIs and Korean officers gained valuable field experience piling tweed jackets behind the station.

Guard took the man to the main cell, a low-ceilinged room where rows of prisoners stayed chained to concrete walls. They faced each other, looking ahead as three guards flanked them. At mealtimes, guards checked whether the prisoners were alive. Prisoners often stood a dead body up in the night, hoping to get an extra serving. Some prisoners had been shipped from Jeju Island, others from Daejeon or the mountains. Guard didn't deny the prisoners were sincere. It was always "Free us, free us" and nothing more, but Verdi understood freedom to be vague and wrote instead about love, absent of intentions. *Amor è palpito dell'universo intero, misterioso, altero, croce e delizia al cor—* Love is a heartbeat throughout the universe, mysterious, altering, the torment and delight of my heart. It was easy to recognize the prisoners and their problems because they didn't want freedom by the end of their torture program; they wanted tenderness, love.

The man wouldn't touch his food, so the other prisoners lunged. The eldest guard shot a hand for moving out of position.

Guard scolded him for wasting bullets.

After mealtime, Guard sat across from the man at his office desk. "Information says you're being transferred to Daejeon Prison. That's not right. They say you live in town with a daughter named Insuk—you're a local. You have service medals."

The man nodded. "You'd be far beneath my station."

"Good. It's the only reason we'd be friends."

"People become friends for less."

Guard chuckled and lit a cigarette. "Friend," he said, "I eat the same prison food as you." He gave the cigarette to the man. "Prisoners complain, but they get out one way or another."

"You're a lifer." The man took a drag with his cuffs on.

The man looked like the conscientious type—the sort who maintained a respectable distance in the bathhouse, scrubbing two seats away, switching from the hot to cold tub if you joined. The sort who starved in a month while in charge of rations. "Clearly, you're not subtle enough to be suspicious. Yet our report says you have a right-wing father. A left-wing maternal aunt."

"Killed by North Koreans."

"Or they're alive in North Korea. You could be talking to them."

"Everybody has family in North Korea. I saw my family die."

"Can you be sure they were killed by North Koreans?"

The question didn't surprise the man. These were the steps of coercive control. Guard took out a tray for him.

The man said, "Our house was ransacked by guerrillas at night."

Guard knew it was the truth. Lies rattled loudly like an empty cart. "The guerillas were starving," Guard said. "All of this is their fault, really."

Guard put out the cigarette.

The man's story was typical among hundreds of interviews. Millhouse owners murdered for their rice. Their mills hollowed out, children found in the snow.

"You wouldn't be sympathetic to their cause," Guard said. "But Information says we've been following you. You're suspected of helping anti-American groups. You're educated. You travel a lot. On what business?"

"Anti-American?" the man said calmly. "Last time I heard, the North's military posed enough of a threat that every South Korean was pro-American."

"You're quick. Americans, well, they aren't very good with their words. They say things without knowing what they mean to us. But the US has been transparent about the importance of keeping military control. We know of their interests on the peninsula."

"Americans had their revolution," the man said. "You'd think they'd let us have ours."

"You're taking a shit right now, aren't you?"

Guard noticed the man's contradictory feelings. The man had to prove his innocence against the urge to do nothing but convict himself in the chair.

Guard agreed with him. "Thirty-five years under Japanese rule." He placed his palms on the edge of the desk. "After the Japanese surrender, a line drawn across the thirty-eighth parallel, designating Soviet and US command over North and South Korea. US military government rule kept Japanese systems in place. The US was against Koreans ruling themselves post-liberation."

"How surprising."

"Democracy doesn't guarantee rapid progress. Americans have backed every major dictator since liberation because Korea isn't ready. There's dirty work to be done. We need to build without distractions."

"So you admit we're obstructed from democracy."

"It's not so simple. College students are brainwashed. They've confused anti-American views with a new outlook toward their North Korean counterparts. They're so anti-American they think the North is their friend. And the North's laughing at us. We have a generation of sympathizers who believe if it weren't for foreigners, there'd be the prospect of national reunification. These kids grow up, what do you think they'll do? They'll open the borders—start us all over."

Outside, spring fleeced with fringe trees. Branches clustered with white flowers, suffused with the boreal light of the river.

"The division of our country was inevitable," Guard said. "Young people don't have immunity. But I don't believe everyone in my prison started as commies. They saw themselves as heroes, harmless. They're commies for sabotaging progress."

"While you provide wanton torture."

Guard wasn't fazed. "I'll give you that. When students walked out during the US occupation, GIs opened fire. Even right-wing Korean police couldn't stomach that," he said. "But reunification is a fantasy, dreamed up by this generation only because there's been no meaningful compromise. We are one people with two fates. Law and order keeps dissidents from dangerous ideas. Commies are not victims or pawns of the US. When all this is over, Koreans will know what is good for Koreans."

"This isn't a country," said the man.

"This isn't a country yet," said Guard.

The man nodded at the Verdi record on the desk. With his wrists bound, he traced letters on the desk's wooden surface. "*Follie. gioir,*" the man said. "Madness, euphoria."

"You know Italian?"

"Madness, euphoria—what's the difference?" the man said. "If madness, then madness. If euphoria, then euphoria."

Guard stared at the invisible lines. He used his palm to wipe the desk where the man had touched. Guard could forgive the prisoners, but who was this man who quoted Verdi? Good and bad men were found everywhere—in all places of society. So it should've been obvious that Guard would one day find in his prison a decent man. Guard waited a minute, then looked at the man. Guard opened his gaze as if bandages of doubt had suddenly fallen from his face. "Did you know," he said to the man, "even heaven has guards."

YOHAN

TORTURE WAS AS OLD as intimacy. I heard water in my ears and followed it south to the coast of Busan, where I'd been just the week before, encountering its waters rushing under the narrow bridges, bubbling in red buckets of clams, splashing from vendor faucets, drip-dropping under eaves of market stalls, swirling in glass mugs of beer, wetting mouths with cider, and squishing inside galoshes, muddying tracks to dock houses, and the plight of the sea bream, cleaved on a wooden block, leaving its spine and shivering eye.

On the second story of a seafood market was a restaurant where I ordered flat fish they sliced into clear slivers on round platters and served with perilla leaves. I placed two slivers on a leaf with raw garlic. Taking it in one bite, I chased it with soju to cut through the sponge of fishiness on my tongue. The restaurant was the only place where I found relief when my limbs stiffened until it pained me to walk around the same time every year.

The owner, a woman in her late forties, touched the tabletop out of respect.

Her husband, an older fisherman, came out of the kitchen with soju. "It's Yohan!" her husband said. "Here's extra, on the house."

"You haven't come by in a while," the owner said. "Help yourself to another bottle. A man can't drink by himself."

"One year today."

"Your wife, I know," she said. "I won't forget it."

"She was young—forty," I said. "I hate to trouble you."

The owner was perceptive. "We're the ones intruding."

"I won't take back a bottle I brought out," her husband said. "You can't dance without drums."

"We'll take the first drink together," she said, "and be out of your way."

I scooped up the bottle before the quick owner had a chance. "I'll do the serving, then it's fair." I poured three glasses. "To the brim. Just for today."

The owner took hers in sips while looking away.

Her husband shot it straight back.

I thought my wife might have been happy to live in the restaurant's upstairs enclave with its polished linoleum floors, heated ondol, threadbare seat cushions. Red chiles and anchovies on woven baskets. Fish on white paper— sunlight on their fins.

"The stew will be out," the owner said before turning to leave, dragging her husband. Then her husband wiped his mouth and slapped her butt. The diners howled.

"The stew will be out two minutes later," said her husband before chasing her into the kitchen. "Maybe I only need one!"

On the drive home, I made a sound in the car no one else could hear—not unlike a sob—as if my body had finally given out after being so tense, the tension building up for these twelve months, hardening into a heavy stone, but the sound stopped as soon as it thumped out of my chest.

The police caught me on the uphill road to my house. When I stepped out, they walked me to their car while rubbing my back, as if to console me. When I tilted my head, water swirled and drummed. Water circled behind my eyes. It passed through the interstitial hallways of my head. Later, as they hosed me down to the bone, I was transfixed by a thought. Guard might be right—love was the highest mark a man could aim for. Yet I couldn't have prepared for love. I found it an uncontrollable stream I could not stop. When my wife and her belly were rushed to the hospital, water soaking her dress and my sleeve, we plumbed through white gowns and whiter rooms, until Insuk crossed the threshold. There was the flame of her fever, swollen fists and pudgy body. Her eyes awake, her pealing sound, and her feet paddling in my palms.

GUARD

GUARD TIPPED OUT THE bucket and waited for the man to wake.

The man's eyes jolted open, sunken and glazed.

"She doesn't need to know," said the man.

"Your daughter. I suspect she's looking for you."

Guard uncuffed the man and traced a word on his palm with his index finger. Guard continued what the man had started, writing, *death*.

Guard offered his palm.

The man wrote on Guard's palm, *life*.

Guard wrote, *man*.

The man wrote, *life*.

Guard wrote, *father*.

The man wrote, *life*.

        traitor.

                life.

        widower.

                life.

        orphan.

                life.

        war.

                life.

        enemy.

life.

country.

life.

division.

life.

destruction.

life.

guard.

The man wrote slower, *life.*

soldier.

life.

son.

life.

friend.

life.

torture.

life.

guns.

life.

prison.

life.

God.

life.

love.

life.

death.

life.

life.

life.

life.

      life.

  life.

      life.

~

GUARD ORDERED THE MAN to be released by morning, and for the first time since he'd taken his post at the prison, Guard slept through the night. He assumed they let the man go without problems, but when Guard came in the next day, he heard the man had been shot to death.

The man had been released as ordered, but one guard felt paranoid it wasn't the actual order given. The order was suspicious. There was no word from Information or the central station. No one could reach Guard as he was sleeping.

So two guards followed the man.

They reported he ran like a rooster who fled the mountain. The two guards, afraid of an error, settled the surest way to handle the situation would be to shoot him in the back.

The man's body was found face down on the street in his pale blue shirt. Guard didn't believe the report of the man running, but it was possible. The detective trusted the report before he read it. The detective said they'd handle the body and the man's daughter. His son-in-law had been hounding the station. His daughter had been seen searching the ICU.

The detective grabbed a bottle of water and drained it. He wiped his mouth and took a breath. "It's only spring, but it's so hot already. This summer's going to be bad, I can feel it. The mosquitoes are having a feeding frenzy on my asshole."

When Guard asked about the man's burial, the detective hollered. "You country folks are so superstitious." He spat on the ground. "I don't believe in any of that stuff."

"I suppose not."

"The guy had no friends. He was probably up to no good on his trip. He should've taken care of it with a hooker."

The detective splashed water on his forehead and chucked the bottle.

"Speaking of which," the detective said, "I need a girl tonight. My wife is at her sister's with the baby. She complains all day. What's so hard about being a woman?"

"We're not in Japan," Guard said. "Don't be so casual about prostitutes."

The detective was thoughtful. "I don't know how Japanese men got their wives to agree to let them have prostitutes after work and after dinner. Korean prostitutes no less." The detective went on, "I took a boat there once, on assignment. Prostitutes are their economy. It lets them work salarymen to death. And men will work harder for sex. They don't call it fucking. They call it healing."

The detective spun his finger above his head, signaling the team to retrieve the body and load it onto the truck. Guard and the detective stood close enough to see the quick rites done over the body before it was covered with a tarp. "That's universal, ask the Americans," the detective said. "Men need this word, *healing*."

The detective ripped off his gloves, tossed them into the truck on top of the tarp. He looked as if he might launch into another tirade, but it must've been too hot.

They had to head back and write separate reports.

After they had taken out the blockage, the road where the man had been shot returned to its natural flow of passersby.

In his report, Guard requested the man be sent to the coroner.

Guard also reported the two guards who had shot the man and the on-site detective as suspicious for commie activity. There was no evidence, only Guard's word on the matter. After sending in his report, Guard felt satisfied they would be imprisoned by morning, and the central station would present him with a reward.

QUICKLY, QUIETLY, the coroner worked. He recognized the man on the table. The coroner notified the man's daughter as soon as they wheeled him in. He wanted to be done before she arrived.

After the coroner cleaned the body, he gathered his supplies. Usually a mortician prepared the body, but it was his job after the pileup from the protests. He drained the body before pumping bright embalming fluid to add color as if the body might still be alive. Setting the features, he closed the eyelids with pins, to create the appearance of sleep. The coroner's powders and makeup sticks were meant for cold skin. His skill and imagination would allow the daughter's visitation to feel intimate—even if that intimacy depended on how well he covered the truth of the damage.

The coroner was surprised by the body's definition. He'd try to describe it to his colleagues. He'd never seen a body in such good condition after being doused with water and shot eight times in the back, five in the front, clean through. The forearms and biceps still contained a rage, rising with nowhere to go. There was a terrible strictness in the musculature, but gorgeous, slender fingers. A sloped neck and jutting chin meant for singing. Before his certification, the coroner was afraid he would no longer feel sad when people died. That he might concern himself with preparation alone. But it was the opposite—he mourned harder. Standing before the body, he grieved for the man as much as he had ever grieved before. The coroner took off his gloves and rubbed his eyes, staring above the door. He was in one of his moods again. It was never the dead causing trouble.

The coroner cleaned his instruments. He made an incision and tensed—a rush of water flooded the table. He opened the body further, carving a slit along its side. Through the pocket, the coroner swore he could see swimming flat fish. The sandstone scales glided beneath the sliver in the skin. They dove and surfaced, their fins glistening.

When he looked again, there was nothing.

The coroner didn't hear the knock and jumped when the door opened. The man's daughter approached. The coroner excused himself and was heading for the door when he glimpsed for the first time how the world did not break all at once but started to crack just as it was doing across the lovely face of that man's daughter, like madness, like euphoria.

4

INSUK

Daejeon, 1982

NOW THAT MY FATHER WAS DEAD, I COULD TELL him anything:

Let me tell you how I decided to speak only when asked a question and not give answers when no question was asked. I pretended my dolls were you and my mother and bashed them together for answers. One day she stepped behind the curtain, and you joined her. The death of my family taught me to be silent, so I've become a listener by trade in my late twenties. People treat me differently. They tell me things they've never told anyone. Sungho's mother, Huran, says I lost my inheritance when your house was ransacked. Your death caused a vacuum, like the coup. Your stolen celadon vases, lacquered tables, linen dragonfly drapes—all the money Huran needs to pay for the wedding.

Huran stares as I change into the green hanbok that belonged to my mother. Huran says green suits pale skin, not like mine. She says my bow flops down like a dog's ears

For the wedding, held in her basement rental, Huran borrows a black jacket and black cotton skirt. She frowns every time the neighbors say we're a handsome pair of newlyweds. After the wedding, she washes and folds her clothes. She returns them neater than when she received them.

I knot my hanbok in a bundle so tight I won't open it ever again.

That night Sungho tells us he has settled on America.

Sungho will leave in the morning. I must stay here with Huran until he can pay to bring us. He says it won't take him a year to call for us, but Huran says it could be two or five or longer.

Sungho finishes packing and we clean the rooms.

Huran prepares her floor pad on the concrete by the kitchen stove in the anteroom so that Sungho and I can spend the first night of our marriage on the ondol-heated floor of the bedroom. Huran says she hopes deep down that I'll refuse the bedroom to save my mother-in-law from the cold kitchen floor. Then Huran prays in the bedroom to give me an hour to consider it. If I were her daughter, she wouldn't have asked me to switch rooms. If she were my mother, it wouldn't have taken me an hour to refuse.

When it comes time, Huran steps through the doorway as if it takes all of her strength to cross the boundary.

It hardly makes sense to stop her. Why should I halt anyone on a path? Who does she expect me to be—this woman who marries without a smile?

Huran asks me, "Are you going to take the bedroom?"

Sungho comes out of the kitchen and says to her, "I got wood for the stove, so it'll be warm."

Huran stays put. "You wouldn't make your father sleep outside."

"It's just for the night," Sungho says.

Huran waits for me to speak. She can't argue with her son without the support of his wife.

But I have no intention of siding with Huran. I ask Sungho, "What do you think?"

Sungho says that we will take the bedroom.

Huran says her son is normally a kind boy. This is her way of insulting me.

"Mom, it's for one night," Sungho says. "After that, you'll have Insuk for yourself."

"This is why children are like tree branches." Huran turns into the kitchen. "The more branches you have, the more wind."

Sungho gathers the hem of my nightgown so I won't have to fuss as we pass through the door that Huran stepped through a second before.

It's Sungho who toes the door closed. But I know Huran suspects me.

The kitchen is only three feet away from where Sungho

and I curl up on the heated linoleum. Mumbling comes through the thin wall. Huran's praying again in the kitchen.

Soon I hear Sungho groaning.

I'll recall our wedding night was supposed to give me hope and carry me through the time that Sungho's gone. The morning light breaks the stillness of the room. The floor pad and blankets and clothes need to be washed, the softness of his body put back into place, the floor wiped with lemon and water. All the rooms of my life held my best and worst memories. The cold splash from our sink, the smell of cooked rice, the table set with camellias and yellow-ringed melons. My mother died in a room, and you lay still in another; I conceived in the room that night, and I'll give birth in yet another, but in every one of the rooms, I dream of the life I am owed.

~

NOW THAT MY MOTHER was dead, she could hear everything:

Let me tell you how Huran runs the chicken coops on a farm owned by the family who lives in the house where she rents the basement. The coops are located three miles on foot along the railroad tracks. Huran pays for space on the farm and keeps the earnings from selling poultry to a restaurant client. Eight months have passed since Sungho left. In a shed behind the coops, Huran and I change into coveralls. She looks at my dark nipples and swollen middle, as if foretelling a difficult future. We put on red aprons and yellow rubber gloves. Huran pushes the top of my belly and pulls the apron ties to meet behind me. She tucks in the loose strands under my hairnet.

With Sungho gone, I suspect we've become closer than we would have otherwise. We live in such close proximity she knows I have to pee just by looking at me. Huran says that without me, Sungho won't come back for her. She also says that without her, I'd probably run away. She sees nothing wrong in saying these things openly. Huran gives me the impression of a cat sprawling in the comfort of any arrangement so long as she can slip in and out of its fences. We bleach the steel tables, sharpen the butcher knives, test the edges. One hundred forty-two chickens huddle in cages at our feet.

The US Army chief of staff declares that Koreans are "field mice," not yet ready for democracy. Field mice or not, we have to work with no word from Sungho since he left the country. I can't worry about what he might be doing. Seeing my belly grow bigger, I feel desperate to kill chickens. So what if the GIs yell *tomodachi* at the children, not knowing it's Japanese? So what if the GIs write letters home that Korea is a vacation with shovels for digging trenches, and brothels for digging girls? If the GIs have no idea what they're supposed to do, maybe nobody does.

I pick up a chicken by its tan wings and lower it onto the table. Gathered with tucked feet, it gives no struggle against the blade's strike. Few flutter off the table, their scabbed feet set loose. I draw back their red-combed heads, holding them with some final ease. I look each one in the eye. Some show they're alive by returning my gaze. It's dirty work, but I feel cleansed by it. I ask for mercy, making quick cuts. The knife sends a voltage through the bird, like the one that breaks through my sleep every morning from the fact that you and my father are dead.

Huran asks me, "Have you talked to Sungho?" She must know the answer since we live together, and back at the basement, she would've noticed me leaving to receive the call at the post office. Huran wants me to feel uncomfortable.

I gather the chicken hearts—their tiny fires—in a bin for the restaurant. I can't believe the heat rising through my gloves.

Huran saws through a cage since the key doesn't work in the broken lock. She pops it open and says, "He's working on his driver's license—you have to drive to get a job in that country."

I bathe the chickens in hot water. I keep my posture straight as I pluck them with one hand and spin them with the other, as if playing a stringed instrument.

Then Huran looks at her bird. "What number are you?" Because she's lost count of the birds, the restaurant will be unhappy with us.

Shrugging, Huran goes on, "Insuk—my son hasn't forgotten about his mother. He writes me and sends me pictures."

I stop because she called me by name. This time is different.

Huran takes a heart out of its gooey film and says, "Your husband's taking driving lessons from a woman—a Korean woman who went to a popular girls' school in Seoul."

My head goes down. I adjust my heavy coveralls.

"You're not a complete idiot, are you? They're spending a lot of time together," Huran says. "I spoke with Sungho, and I have my suspicions."

I hand the naked birds over to be gutted, and all I say to her is, "I suppose it would've happened sooner or later."

"You know what this means for both of us." Huran hangs a braid of guts on the line and sprays it with water. She turns to me, and says, "You're with his child."

"Do you want me to be angry with him?"

I feel bitter she's told me about the woman, and I speak freely now that we've been living together.

"Maybe you'd like me to leave him."

Huran removes her gloves and wipes her hands. "Even a worm wiggles when you step on it." She fetches a folded photograph out of her pocket. "You're more pathetic than I thought. See for yourself!"

The photograph has traveled across the ocean.

"Your husband got a new car, too," she says, "and no doubt he can start his new life with it." Huran starts on a pile of slain chickens, splayed into hunks. She asks, "What do you see in that picture?"

"Your son."

"In that picture," she says, "he's your husband."

Then I notice a woman standing next to Sungho.

"The driving instructor," I say.

"Her hair is too long to be trusted." When I see Huran shaking, I realize she must fear that her son is out of her reach.

The driving instructor stands close to him. They hug each other when they have no idea that once you pick up an affair, you can't set it back down. Huran jumped at the chance to show me.

"I don't know what to say to you, child," and Huran re-gloves. She wipes the steel counter and unfurls from her fingers a tangle of organs—purses of blue and green.

I touch the photograph before going back to work.

We prepare the innards and the fleshy jackets. Hose out the freezer boxes and load them into the refrigerator. Fill the last ones, cover them in ice and plastic. The sun dips on a scrim between the farmhouse doors and the hill, telling us to drop our work. Huran watches me clean the tables and instruments while stinking of blood that a hard rain can't get rid of.

Huran says to me, "She's not half as pretty as you, Insuk. Don't cower like an idiot. You get on the phone at the post office, and you ask for Sungho and talk to him. You do it tonight—don't let him sleep well. Do you understand? You tell him you're his wife and you have his child. You tell him if this bitch is teaching him anything other than driving, you'll cut him. My husband beat me, but he didn't cheat on me because he knew I'd stab him in his sleep. This is what your mother was supposed to tell you. Don't let your husband get away with this, or you'll have to kill him. You will never forgive yourself if you don't straighten this out right away. Do it now. Tell him there are boys and girls dying in this country, crying from church to church, running from school after school, filling prison after prison. Tell Sungho I'm ashamed of him and he should do more for a woman like you, working at the farm with his old mother and these poor chickens. Tell him I showed you the picture and tell him how useless this instructor is and how stupid he looks standing next to her."

~

MOTHER, FATHER:

Let me tell you how the following week we hear students set fire to the US Cultural Service Building in Busan while people watched the explosion from the road. Plumes of smoke. Church bells ringing. Dogs with their heads cocked, circling. The extremists, arrested. Death sentences. Students dousing the American flag with petrol. Fires spreading. Those fires calling to other fires in other parts of the country. News on the wind like a ship hull of memory. The US ambassador warns "spoiled" Koreans against their view of history. Japanese textbooks say Japan "advanced," not "invaded," the Korean peninsula.

The restaurant client praises our tidy work.

The chickens were shipped in exact batches. One hundred forty-two chickens. They ask to increase our shipments.

There's recognition in Huran's eyes over the profits. It's double pay for us, and the leftover chicken hearts they didn't want will feed us.

Huran says she can't complain. "Everybody has a dead son but me," she says. "And now we'll eat better than anyone."

"I can sell the hanbok, too."

"Then we have to buy it again," she says. "Forget it."

"We can add a client. Anybody would hire us."

"Even if we're all idiots," she says, "running around with our heads cut off."

"Don't forget our small hearts."

Huran laughs. "Poor chickens."

We squat at the stove to boil water and warm our hands. The flames lick our fingertips. Light skews across our faces. The pot simmers as Huran seems to try and articulate a question.

Huran watched me march into the post office and return with a confidence worn like a new coat. Though her concerns about the instructor made sense, they were exaggerated. Sungho reassured me he would call for us at the end of the month. Huran doesn't say a word, but I sense she's focused on something. From the changes taking place in front of me, I feel terrified of what might happen to us. Our shared circumstances gave Huran and me a common goal and distracted us from each other. Now we had to fly six thousand miles away from the room where we finally came together.

Huran slides veggie scraps into the water, a few hearts, and works up the nerve.

"What's it like?" she asks. "Sleeping with my son?"

I'm thoughtful, laughing softly.

Huran can't help but feel curious.

I reach out to strangle a neck. "It's a little like killing chickens."

~

LET ME TELL YOU how at twenty-seven, I step into the light of April 1983 in Northern California—arriving in a country that calls itself united when not even the seasons unite them. Fumes from a landfill, collecting waste for the region, scorch the Milpitas air. America has many faces. The elderly who slump over like ripe wheat in the doorways. Foothills golden in the sun. Static air from the salt marshes. Streets named after creeks: Coyote Creek, Hidden Creek, Canyon Creek. I'm here one day, and I already miss the sun banking through the gates of our house. But it never occurred to me that when I arrived at the airport, Sungho—the same man with spectacles in a short-sleeve shirt—would take his mother's bag and seat her up front. The baby and I fold into the back. Huran grins so wide you can hang a laundry line on her lips. You might say it's natural for a mother to envy her son's wife, and for her son to treat his wife differently in front of his mother, but I was fooled. As we pass over the bridge, Sungho and I might as well be taking our last breaths as newlyweds.

Sungho assures Huran I won't be trouble for her. His words are deliberate—his manner seems an accusation. Sungho says he has no time to settle our quarrels because of his job at the dry cleaners. His face goes still in the rearview mirror, his gaze older than a second before. Perhaps it's this look, between Sungho and me, when he sees me for the first time since he left and does not take one step toward me, that I feel the time that's passed between us. Let me tell you how I pinch Henry's leg—the leg of an innocent soul—and how the five-week-old wails in the car. Let me tell you how the sound startles Sungho and Huran. They peer into his knotted face the way they peered into mine and gave me hope to the last minute. Henry's piercing cry gives me palpable relief from the pent-up pressure in my chest. I comfort Henry to soothe his need for his mother, and soothe my need for mine. How many times would Henry have to feel this discomfort before he understood me? Why do I want him, just a baby, to meet me where no one else can—a baby I carry in my arms like a Bible?

II

ANIMAL KINGDOM

1988–1997

5

HENRY

San Jose, 1988

I WAS FIVE WHEN I RODE WITH MY MOTHER TO HER work on the other side of the world. Biwon was a Chinese Korean restaurant in a narrow plaza on El Camino, where my mother waited tables with girls in black dresses and black stockings and black heels. The girls complained about the high cost of dry cleaning but said the California economy was strong with innovation and air-choking smog. So the girls paid to look tidy and served oily fried pork, crackling rice soup, spicy seafood noodles, and their specialty, red pepper drumsticks, to churchgoers and drunks. There were four private dining rooms in addition to the main restaurant. My mother put me in one of the empty rooms, as if a son was a kite you had to tie down. It wasn't like being at home where I'd run my hands along the walls and see myself sailing across their white expanse—where imagined things looked more real than reality. She warned me, "Biwon is the most real thing in the world," and I didn't see her again until closing.

The rulers of the Biwon kingdom, a plump and soft-spoken husband and wife, were calm because they'd never had children. They ruled by standing taller around the girls, like a boa constrictor stretching out next to you to measure whether you'd fit inside its belly if it swallowed you. Since they cooked without concern for the customers' health, they were popular. The wife said to me, "You want to live a little, then you want to die a little. That's why my cooking's better than your mom's." The rulers called my mother delicate like the pale noodles they rolled with thick-sauced jjajang as black as her dress. When she was alone, I saw my mother's eyes—two glistening pools in the dark—as she soothed herself, her mouth a fold of flesh. Biwon trapped her by paying in cash. She told me I couldn't understand money because I was five. I drew simple shapes, I read simple books. Maybe my mother had to be right—she couldn't take a single step out of Biwon for fear of being wrong.

On the staff's lunch break, I knocked on the back door of Biwon where a server, Jinju, let me in with a cackle, teasing me in her country voice. "You can tell a promising tree from just a sapling." Jinju was a college student with round cheeks and brown eyes. From behind her, the smells of Biwon greeted me in the hallway. The air was thick with boiling jam and the bitter scent of coffee. I heard the sounds of heels crossing the minimal interior, dimly lit by lamps. News about the 1988 Summer Olympics in Seoul kept the girls arguing. They took sides according to their wages. Jinju and a few others opposed the Olympics, saying it'd further division because North and South Korea couldn't jointly host the games. Jinju crossed her stockinged legs and slurped black noodles through painted lips.

The rumors about Biwon were true—the girls were pretty. Illicit moles drawn by their eyes and their slim necks. Jinju said, "American imperialism forces the Korean government to keep the separation. It's not a natural division but a strategic one." She poured herself coffee. "Being human in the current world is to ignore what happens at the borders of nations." My mother and the larger group disagreed. Students were marching for a joint host, but demonstrations went too far. Students ought to study, not arm themselves. I heard my mother say the same thing she'd told me that morning. "Throwing firebombs into the road? You're cursed by your imagination," she said, holding her cup in both hands. "Things are different in reality." On the television behind her, Michael Jackson shrugged and pointed down.

Jinju's boyfriend came after lunch with an extra pair of stockings, like he did every week, and disappeared with her into the dining room closet. From outside the doors, I heard him compliment her grip. Listening so intently to the rhythmic drums inside the closet, I felt my breath building up to theirs. Her boyfriend stepped out, then Jinju. I gazed at the energy in the curves of her wrists as she patted my cheek and brought me to life. When she embraced me at the night's end, my heart weakened and I felt a temper in my pants. If I drew a picture, it'd look like a crooked nose. I once overheard Jinju's boyfriend ask her what her favorite movie was, and Jinju told him *All Quiet on the Western Front*. "War makes me feel helpless," she said. There must've been a higher place she yearned to reach, and helplessness was a path to that place.

~

ONE AFTERNOON AT BIWON, Jinju directed two men out of the parking lot dust and into a private room. She had on invisible stockings—seen only by the concentric sheen on her thighs. My mother served the men, who had gold watches and greased shoes, and I listened from under the table. Mansae, the older one, owned the Korean supermarket on El Camino. Robert, the younger one, invested in cafés along the same strip. Robert spoke perfect English and used words like *suffocating* and *progress*. In Robert's boyhood photographs he must've looked as he did now—a man in a gray suit who had aged ahead of time in his clothes. When Robert waved, an ashtray appeared. My mother's footsteps went to and from the table. Robert sat with his feet firmly apart, facing the kitchen. Robert folded his hands over his lap, and when she shuffled away, his elbows hit the tabletop.

"Let it go, Robert. Nobody gets apologies," Mansae said.

"The German chancellor laid a wreath at the memorial of the Warsaw Ghetto. Brandt actually kneeled."

"What's the use in hoping Japan will ever kneel—and on what memorial? The sushi guys at Yaohan are nice to us. That's good enough."

"Brandt fell to his knees in '70." Robert leaned forward and tipped the round table off its center leg. "It was a sign of atonement. There were big problems. But in the next ten years, we're looking at German reunification."

Mansae locked his ankles together. "That's a leap. It was polarizing."

"You sound like a typical politician."

"I know Mitterrand and Kohl held hands in Verdun '84."

"So you think you've seen it all?"

Robert put in an order for onions, but Mansae canceled it.

"We need to head out," Mansae said. "You're giving me a headache."

"People everywhere keep that photograph of Brandt. You know why? They need to see it for themselves. A world leader, kneeling. It's the most important gesture in history."

"Japan won't do it. They won't kneel in a thousand years."

They touched teacups. "Not in a million," they said.

"It wouldn't be enough, anyway," Robert said. "People who didn't suffer through the war have no real sense of when it began and when it ended."

"Who cares? The commies were the problem."

"North Koreans still live with the horrors of Japanese colonialism. They're also the victims of the worst carpet-bombing in history. US dropped more bombs over North Korea than during the entire World War II Pacific campaign, including napalm. Of course the North is a postcolonial state. Of course they can't trust the world. They hate everyone because their kids were melting on the ground."

"They're not my kids," Mansae said.

"My point." Robert scribbled on the bill. "The real commies were safe in private bunkers."

"What're you doing now?"

"I didn't stay this long for you."

"You mean the waitress?" Mansae chuckled. "Who's going to put up with you? They'd have to follow you around apologizing every second."

After the two men left, I dashed out from under the table. My mother caught me, but I noticed in her other hand, she was carrying the bill. On it was the signed receipt and several hundred dollars of tip with a note. I followed my mother, who forgot to reprimand me, to the kitchen and heard her insisting on splitting the tip with Jinju. My mother was thirty-two and I knew the smallest things could darken her mood, but in the kitchen that night, her face lightened and her fingers touched her lips as if her whole outlook had changed. My mother loosened her grip on me, her finger and thumb barely looped around my wrist.

ROBERT SAT AT THE same air-conditioned table for a smoke, a rest from the stagnant California air, and asked for my mother, who served him without change in her footsteps or her voice. He spoke to her about what it was like to lose willpower, to be brutalized, to be condemned to a place one did not feel responsible for. Jinju pinched my mother to stop sharing her tips. "When you have no money, you give it away without a care," Jinju said. "But when you're rich, you'll regret you ever did."

My mother told the girls something I'd heard for the first time—that as a girl she had protested the GIs in her hometown. The girls, shocked, needled her, making her laugh. My mother confessed she felt nostalgic seeing the student activists—and men like Robert, whose visits became more frequent. One day I asked Robert to show me his hand. I wrote with the tip of my finger *Henry*. At five, I was late in learning how to spell, but Robert said with proper schooling, even a dog could recite a poem. Robert asked me for a word that I'd like to spell. I asked for his name, and he put his finger on my palm: *Freedom*.

Jinju told my mother in private, "You must never forget Robert isn't one of us. He's a terrifying man." I felt excited to hear such a thing, but my mother grew older—parallel lines cutting across her forehead, her eyes squeezing out tears like the juice from ripe fruit—and she drove home and locked herself in the bedroom she shared with my father. I wondered if childhood ever ended. I reassured my mother through the crack in the door that none of it had to be real.

~

THE FIRE BEGAN IN the kitchen and spread west to the restaurant's front exterior, withering the decorative bushes while it was dark outside. The restaurant sign, engulfed by the flames, lolled off the roof like a tongue out of its head. I was in the waiting area when my mother saw smoke from the kitchen. Three cooks flew out, and my mother grabbed me. From the karaoke bar and video rental shop in the same plaza, choking workers lunged through the doors and out into the open air. My mother counted those who piled out. The cooks, who tried to confront the fire, inhaled smoke and singed their lungs. Embers the size of insects, then the size of animals, devoured the restaurant. The wind picked up and the flames danced wildly. The fire trucks came. Then ambulances and police cars. No one talked to the authorities. There was nothing to say—only a boy in the distance baying like a dog.

They found that the fire had been ignited by cooking oil and parchment in the kitchen. It spread when the ductwork, exhaust systems, and vents behind the stove sucked up the flammable vapors, and smoke took to the grease buildup. The oven hoods and steel appliances were filthy since the porters weren't paid enough to be responsible. The porters skipped chores and ducked into the karaoke bar to drink soju for two bucks a bottle. The rulers didn't bother with in-depth cleaning of the fire-safety systems since it cost as much as a deluxe dinner set for thirty or forty guests, and the price was hiked for larger establishments like Biwon. The rulers said it happened because it'd been the hottest season we ever had, fueled by the sin of industrial waste. Prayers came out of their mouths to a God who would keep us here.

~

NO ONE CARED ENOUGH to stay during Mass to pray for Biwon—for fear of missing the opening ceremony of the Seoul Olympics, shown on the television in the church's auditorium. The churchgoers funneled out of the worship room after Eucharist. The grandmothers let out their coughs. The altar boy still had on his robe. In the auditorium, we poured soju bombs, sikhye for the children. My mother, out of a job, sat with me on the parquet floor. We formed a half circle around the screen with my father and grandmother and a crowd of others—quieter now than during the raising of the wine goblet during Mass. Our concentration wouldn't have broken if a fire truck had driven straight through the auditorium. It was so still you might as well have shot a gun into the air.

I focused on the screen, taking in the excitement, the spectators waving flags in the stands. Bright-colored feathers on the green field. My mother was in a daze, resting her chin on her knees. The Olympics let us imagine ourselves rising above life's conditions.

The doves appeared. They were released as a symbol of world peace. When the cages opened, the doves were supposed to fly off on their ivory wings. They were supposed to be a fond public memory—our turned-true dreams.

Many doves landed on the ring of the Olympic cauldron. The spectators laughed at the madness of perching on a cauldron. Then I recognized what could happen.

"Mom, don't look."

"Are you scared, Henry?"

I told her the ceremony wouldn't go as planned.

"It's all in your head," she said.

The athletes raised their torches to the cauldron. Fire came alive only as something was consumed.

The fire touched the ring and zipped to the farthest end. We held our breath, willing the doves to float off from the heat. But the doves stayed where they were perched. Their shadows thinned to blades. Waning, blotted, then gone. A sharp cry in the auditorium confirmed what we saw. Our dream took another shape among the flames, with no sign of struggle, as if it had never existed. Throughout the auditorium, the churchgoers paced the floor. When I saw the spectators looking up at the sky, I understood that people prayed because they could not free themselves. The doves were a memory that had to be erased—a memory that had to be forgotten in our soft, closed palms. So few would recall the lighting of the Olympic cauldron where the doves burned alive.

~

ON A FRIDAY TWO years after the Olympics, I was seven and sitting in the Hankook Market food court, where my mother batter-fried me squid legs. When Robert found me, I told him my age without using my fingers. Robert took me to the loading dock and told me to hold out my hands but no peeking. Something heavy closed the space in my arms. I locked my fingers to keep it against my chest. Opening my eyes, I met a dog whose paws rested in the air. Just twelve pounds, the dog fit perfectly in my arms. The dog was a short-haired terrier with pointy ears, a stout body, and bright eyes. He was black with tan eyebrows, and he smelled like the ocean. The dog sniffed me, nose tugging, and I loved the dog with my whole heart.

Robert folded the box he'd brought the dog in and tossed it over the dock. "He's an older guy," he said. "But this is a country where the dogs are happy their whole lives."

I brushed the dog's broad back. "We can learn to talk to each other." The dog glanced at me approvingly.

Robert looked impressed, but a little serious. "He's still a dog. You don't want a dog thinking he's not a dog."

I considered this for a moment. "A dog can say things without talking at all," and I put my face close to the dog's. The dust that swirled around us at the dock had once been a restaurant with girls and cooks, or doves flapping their wings in the air, or whispers and laughter and clapping, or oven hoods and firebombs, or soju and prayers, or televisions and apologies and waving flags, weighing less in the sun as they veered toward and away from us, and all that hope vanished into my next words. "Can I call you Toto?"

TOTO

FROST CAME TO THE tops of the trees. When Toto
sneaked out under the gate, the neighborhood kids chased
him. So Toto went back to the boy. The boy was gentle in
feeding him before going out the door. The boy's father left
rice on the floor and switched on the noisy box. The boy's
mother gave Toto dried fish and asked questions about the
boy. The grandmother hid from Toto, which Toto permit-
ted. Toto knew it was noon by the boy's scent at the door.
When the boy appeared, Toto pushed him down. The boy
stroked Toto's side. "I want to be like you, Toto." They
stretched out in a sunny spot on the floor. Then the boy
rolled over. "Don't worry, Toto. I've got a plan for us." The
boy packed his pockets with fruit. The napkins bruised
with blueberries.

Toto and the boy walked to the fields, where they
hunted rabbits and squirrels. Toto and the boy followed
a hawk to an empty rabbit's nest. They spotted a hornet, a
warning, and changed direction. Chewing long grass, they
rested outside a fox den. They split the berries and turkey
slices the boy had taken from the house. The boy, watching
Toto, devoured his meal off the ground like a dog.

They jumped when a squirrel showed itself. The boy
stilled and said that a squirrel would act differently
whether they responded as a disturbance or a presence. It

was a compliment if the squirrel ignored them. Then the squirrel ran past them. They tracked it to where the cars reared their metal faces. The boy turned back around to the field and Toto followed. "That was close," the boy said. "I can't feel my heart." He pressed his ear against Toto's chest. "There it is. You've got both of ours in there."

The boy found a rock and sat on it. He took out a pad of paper and showed it to Toto. "We're here. These are the nests we found today. This is the trail home. This is where the cars are. Here is the market square." The boy stood and looked around, squinting. "The scale is accurate." The boy changed the orientation of the pad. He drew fruits and trees and insects. "This is what I learned today," he said. "I'm your student, Toto. You can teach me anything."

Back at the apartment, the boy's mother tried to wash him, but he refused until she agreed to wash Toto with him. The boy scolded his mother, "Toto cares about me!"

Afterward, the boy took more turkey slices. They ate them off the floor. Their hairs dripping water, the boy said, "Now I see. I can taste better this way. The food is closer to my nose. If I close my eyes, I can taste it without eating it."

One day, the boy came home carrying a pile of heavy books. They looked dangerous, but his mother was happy to see them.

The boy said he was going to learn how to communicate with animals.

The boy tore out a page and put it in his pocket. He sat cross-legged on the sidewalk in front of the apartment. Toto sensed the boy's concentration.

Toto stayed beside him.

When the boy looked up, Toto looked also.

"Elephants stomp their feet to talk to each other. Frogs make drill sounds. Dolphins use sonar." The boy stomped his feet over the ground. He pushed out his lips and made a noise. Closing his eyes, the boy clapped his hands. "I can tell, I can tell—you're right there," the boy said. "I got two ears and two nostrils like you, Toto."

The boy told him, as Toto rolled onto his side, that he had found a part of Toto the boy hadn't known was there. The boy said Toto acted the way Toto was supposed to. The boy wanted to release Toto from these expectations. The boy saw in Toto his real self—slipping past his best pretenses to be a mere dog.

The boy wanted to free Toto from the roles put on his kind. "Nobody's ever asked you about yourself. Of course you don't want to say anything. Maybe it's been so long you forgot how to talk. But I can wait for you, Toto. Forever."

Toto was pleased with the boy's excitement.

The boy closed the book. "If I could ask you anything? Huh. I guess—did you have fun with me today?"

Toto lay on his back, the sun on his belly.

"Did you say something?"

Toto licked his lips—he was tired. Toto had been an old dog when he met the boy.

"Toto, do you love me?"

Toto, for the first time, felt a strong sensation from the boy. Toto recalled the feeling he'd had when he was tied outside for a long time. Toto rested his head on the boy.

"You make everything better, Toto. I don't know what I'd do without you. If you ran away, you would come back, right? You would come back because you have a good home."

The boy took his paw and drew a picture of them. An easy stillness fell around the sidewalk, and the sun was gobbled up by the horizon.

Toto licked the boy's face. The boy fell back in surprise and, laughing, scooped Toto up in his arms. "You always kiss me. Did you know, Toto?" he said. "You can't kiss yourself, except in a mirror!" They went outside and slept under the night sky, warm air passing over them. "I've been waiting for you my whole life, Toto." The boy's longing for Toto was an inseparable part of the boy. His longing had a scent, and it was how Toto knew him by heart.

~

TOTO AND THE BOY played in the back seat as the boy's mother drove.

When the car stopped, his mother stepped out.

The car was still running.

Toto saw her rush into a building, waving at them to hurry. Then the boy stepped out and closed the door.

Toto was alone in the car.

When Toto jumped onto the window, there was a loud click inside the car. The boy looked back at Toto.

All of a sudden the boy ran to the car. It was summer and Toto could see the heat rising off the ground.

"Toto!" The boy tried the door handle.

The boy's mother appeared.

"Toto locked himself in!"

"Oh my God," and his mother pushed him aside.

His mother rushed into the building again. The boy banged on the window.

Toto panicked. He hopped between the front and back seats.

"Don't run around, Toto!" said the boy. "Just hold on!"

A man, whom the boy called Robert, rushed out of the building. "The fire department put us on hold."

The boy's mother asked the man, "How long does Toto have?"

"A few minutes," said the man. "You should've told Henry to wait in the car."

"He's not a normal boy—he does whatever he wants," said his mother.

Toto circled the front seat and found a spot to lie in.

The man stood above the window and fiddled with the door.

Toto barked at the man. The boy started to cry. "Toto has thick fur. If it's too hot for me, I know he's burning up inside."

Toto looked at the boy, looked at the door.

The man rolled his shirtsleeves, sweating.

After a while, the man smiled. "I got it."

Just then Toto jumped onto the window again and, at the same time, there was another loud click inside the car.

"What was that?" The boy's mother let go of him.

"Toto unlocked himself," the boy said.

The man opened the door and yanked Toto out by the scruff. Toto couldn't stand on his own.

The boy carried Toto inside the building, where there was a bowl of cold water. The boy told him eleven minutes had passed.

The man yelled at Toto, and the boy laughed.

"Just send the fire trucks back." The man took his shirt off.

His mother thanked the man, and the boy did too.

The boy rubbed Toto. "I was so scared, Toto."

"This dog," the man said. "He won't live forever. Your mom says he's a lot of trouble."

"Toto's a good dog. He saved himself."

"Is that right?" The man rubbed his face, then crouched down and said to Toto, "You better live a long time, or it'll be a waste of a good boy."

~

ONE MORNING AFTER THE cold season came and went, Toto found a quiet spot on the sidewalk. It was a place where he could stay and breathe softly and lie still. Toto had always known these things to make sense. When the boy's mother found him, she brought him to a place where there was a white room. They put him in a cage with a pad underneath, ripped up by other dogs. Toto was getting tired, and if he wanted to, he could sleep. Toto planned to do just that but hadn't seen the boy.

The boy's father came and dropped off Toto in another white room. It was bigger and brighter. They put Toto on a table where he waited for the boy. They put things before his eyes, but Toto didn't pay them any attention. More time went by. Toto waited until noon, when the boy's mother showed up again.

"Something we do," they said, "is check if his eyes follow anything in front of him. If he's interested, or if he's just there but not looking at us."

The boy appeared in the doorway.

Toto looked up for the first time, and the boy looked at him.

"These things," they said, "they happen so fast in smaller dogs. There are little signs to go by, and by the time we notice them, it's hard to turn things around."

The boy's mother picked him up. "I'm so sorry, Toto."

Toto was comfortable—his gaze went up to hers.

"I didn't know, Toto," she said. "I shouldn't have worried so much. I should've thanked you for loving my son instead."

She passed Toto to the boy.

Leaving his mother with the people in the white room, the boy took Toto to the car.

The boy was distraught. He put Toto on his lap. "You don't smell like yourself, Toto. You're a little sour." Toto's head rested comfortably on the boy's arm. "We can't fix everything for you. You have to want to stay with us, Toto. You do want to stay, don't you?"

The first notes of sleep fell on Toto, touching his eyes.

"I don't have anybody but you," and the boy started to shake.

Toto's breathing slowed. His fur sank into his ribs.

Now the boy seemed to understand. Toto wanted the boy to see for himself what Toto had accepted a long time ago, and if Toto could do it, then he was sure the boy could do it too.

"Toto, don't go. Please stay." The boy rocked him. "It's not real, Toto. It's not happening, Toto."

Here they were together, their seeing eyes, serious ears. Here were the months they spent in the weather, the barns and fields, the cars and rooms, and their looks that touched one another, as if each were a lake connected by their reflections and hidden in one was a part of the other. Here they'd gone down the road and past the traffic signal, curved toward the narrow path along the fields. Here they counted moths and covered wells and glass bottles. Here they listened to the footsteps of an ant. Here they dressed as piles of leaves, eschewing the light so it could not reach them, and here the sound had gone but the world could still be seen. Here was their gumption and silliness. Here the boy cried as he said things he didn't mean, like he never knew what Toto was feeling, and Toto recognized that tinge in his own chest. Here the boy said he loved him, and it was a thing so obvious, it never had to be uttered except to prepare them for when it couldn't be told again. Here they slowed to a routine of a tiny scale, testing the rise and fall of their breaths, because they were routinely tied together.

Here Toto was going to show the boy the edge of their real imaginings. The body that does not die is not a body, and Toto was pleased to bound ahead of the boy on another path. Before the boy's mother returned, Toto left his eyes open—an empty gaze—so the boy could see him the way they had met, face to face, but also know that Toto was different. The fuzz on Toto's corneas, the absence of him blinking, his stillness sucking up air. Toto was now in the fields with the mice and the hawks and the rabbits and the foxes and the insects and the fruits and the sun. Toto was in an owl pellet they'd opened together, he was the bones, beaks, and fur. He was their bright and curious joy. From them, nothing could be taken away. The fields and the farmhouses and the animals could disappear. The dust they recognized so well could gallop and the mice could scatter and the cobwebs could fill room after room. Here was Toto joined to the boy like a wish because Toto, for the boy, could wait forever.

6

INSUK

Milpitas, 1992

OUR TOWNHOME STUCK OUT FARTHER THAN
the one attached to it and faced the street at the second
speed bump of the housing complex, where it stood like a
tall, narrow cabinet. It was a newly built townhome four
miles away from the single-bedroom apartment we had
lived in for almost a decade through heat waves and earth-
quakes. Next to the front door was a panel of dappled glass
scattering light. The living room had a modest brown carpet. All walls had windows with sun. Squinting, I passed
into the kitchen and dining area. There was a stove and

sink, a half-circle dining table pushed against the wall. The red floor of the kitchen shone the brightest midday and led to a patio, where Huran lined her milk crates for potting aloe and roses. I could go there to be alone after everyone had fallen asleep, while crickets scratched the wood, and the concrete slab of the patio would reflect the moon's spotlight on me. I was thirty-five. You wouldn't notice the rise of my belly at twelve weeks—my baby the size of an egg.

We chose the townhome for the second floor.

Everyone had a bedroom upstairs. The floor was divided into three rooms. My room with Sungho, and one each for Henry and Huran.

After a short climb of stairs, the bathroom on the left had a tub you could sit in without folding your legs. On the same side was the master with a large window. The room was private. On the right, the two smaller rooms shared a thin wall.

It was obvious that because of the shared wall, Sungho, Henry, and I would take the rooms to the right. Otherwise I couldn't cough or have gas without Huran knowing. Privacy for husband and wife also took priority in my mind. The distance spared Huran and me the embarrassment of my wedding night with Sungho. Henry wouldn't mind his parents because he was nine. And Huran staying on the other side relieved me from bowing so often in my own home.

On moving day, Huran paced from room to room. "Are you putting me in the biggest room in the house?"

"That works well for everyone," I said.

Huran stopped me. "I'm staying in the smaller room."

I wasn't sure what bothered her about the master. I had forfeited the master so Huran could have her space. "We don't have to live on top of each other. We'll have a hallway between us."

Huran stood between the smaller rooms. "You and Sungho will take the first small room. I'll take the second."

I considered the master. The window faced east with a glimpse of the patio. The smaller rooms faced west to the street with the noise of cars and the sight of new construction on the hills.

"The master has privacy and fits a comfortable bed," I said. "If you want, we can take the master." The master would give me privacy, a hallway apart from Huran and Henry.

"You divided the floor between us," Huran said. "You want to put me alone."

Over the years, we had traded sharp looks, and now, standing there between the doors, she reminded me of a child. In the light, not a single line on her face.

I reasoned with her, "Sungho can't be a husband, sharing a wall with his mother."

Huran walked into the master. We peered out the window. Every townhome had a patio with a laundry line hanging with bedsheets and clothes. Neighbors hovered over plants with watering cans. "I refuse to have to step around you to go near my son," she said.

Huran tapped the floor with her foot, as if calling an animal to attention. "I was too kind to you from the beginning," she said. "Sungho's working late since you've gotten pregnant, so maybe you think it's okay to do as you like. Maybe you think you can persuade him to find his mother her own place and finally push me out of the house."

My eyebrows lifted toward the skylight.

I already knew Huran wanted to be near Sungho. From these words, it seemed she also didn't want me to be too close to him, fearing she would lose us both.

Huran followed me downstairs. Standing together in the cramped kitchen, I was struck by how much smaller she'd become as she spread her aged fingers to reach the cupboards. I recalled my mother was significantly taller than her. I prepared an afternoon snack for Henry as he'd be home from school. I took out the rice and rinsed it, let it swell in the water.

I found a pan and cracked two eggs into it.

"You may pat yourself on the back for being his wife," she said. "But if your mother were alive, she'd tell you it means nothing to be his wife in front of his mother."

I breathed deeply, and my shoulders dropped. "How about we ask Sungho when he gets home?"

"A daughter-in-law without a son," she said, "is like a pit without a fire."

The third egg cracked on its own.

Peeling the shell back, I almost dropped it on the floor. Huran looked over and jumped back with a yelp. Cradled inside the shell was a fully formed baby bird.

AFTER LEAVING HENRY WITH Huran at the town-home, I counted my toes and fingers, like a person trying to remember. I drove to the supermarket where I worked a mile down the road from where Biwon used to be on El Camino. Four windows loomed in the storefront—it was closed and dark inside. The red carpet at the entrance like rolled fruit leather. The white fixtures lit up in parts, reaching the corners, the warehouse loading dock, until the whole space was announced. Towers of produce and kitchen supplies, fabrics and heated blankets, videocassettes and stationery. Beveled ceilings and exposed beams. The hum of fridges down the aisles. A figure stood at the food counter.

Robert was two years older than me but looked in his twenties in jeans and a tee. For years, he'd never asked for anything but my company. The nature of our relationship was innocent; I'd never seen him without his suit on. My first impression of him had been of a man so slight and shapeless I was stunned to see him standing there, like a blossom in the winter. I was so surprised I couldn't use my voice. He led me inside to where we wouldn't be seen. I realized, over the years, I had become accustomed to him being close.

"I thought it was you," Robert said.

My shirt clung to my midsection. I sank onto the barstool at the counter under the distilled light.

Robert seemed to sense something was wrong but had no urgency. He moved as if he'd chosen this path himself. "I bought the place from Mansae. I come here whenever I want."

"It's outside of your normal investments."

"You had nowhere else to go but work, huh?"

I fell quiet and watched him grind whole beans, adjust the settings. Dosing the coffee, he cleared the grounds on the portafilter, tamped it down, connected it to the machine.

"What do you think of Henry's father?" I asked him.

This seemed to intrigue him. "Sungho?" He engaged the water pressure, and striped tan-and-brown espresso poured out. "Fighting in a marriage is like cutting water with a knife," he said. "No matter what, it just goes back to how it was before, like nothing happened."

Robert poured the milk, then passed me the cup. He sipped his drink and looked at me. I felt the light of his attention.

"Sungho has no sense of himself," he said. "He only thinks about what he's supposed to do. The world's black-and-white to him. It'll take him lifetimes to figure out."

"If he's not working, he's watching TV."

"You know why the TV was invented?" Robert put his elbows on the counter. "So presidents can apologize in person. The high resolution is so we can see their tears."

The fridges hummed louder.

Robert dug into his pocket and took out my tube of lipstick. "You left it in your apron out back."

I downed the last of my coffee. "I don't look alive with-out it," I said. "Probably good enough for a mortician."

Robert opened the cap. He twisted out the rouge.

Then gestured for me to lean over.

Holding my chin, he filled my lips in. I pressed them together—he cleaned the line of my bottom lip.

"It's not just Sungho," he said. "The fact that an invisible line cuts across our country—that makes the world black-and-white. So he's split down the middle even at home."

Robert had arrived on El Camino in 1980 at twenty-five to buy and sell businesses, and round up like-minded indi-viduals. He ran for mayor as an independent and came in sixth, then founded the daily paper *Liberation Shinmun* for activists, defectors, and their families—arguing in its pages with historians, philosophers, and prime ministers. But reunification was an impossible jigsaw. "The fact that the line exists at all concerns the rest of the world. It's proof of our inhumanity," he said. "Reunification can start here with us."

"But the ones who came here," I said. "We don't even like each other. Back home, we wouldn't be friends. Here, we're friends because we have to be. Everyone has to be family. And you can't choose family." I looked at him as if studying an unopened envelope. "Ideas of reunification died with people like my father. Let them stay dead."

"Reunification can be a reimagination." Robert raised his fingers. "One country, two systems."

"Sungho's afraid people like you will start another war. I don't know exactly what reunification means. It's already vague, but the bigger problem is whether people want to be united at all. It's easier to unite criminals. They know what they want, and they work together to get it. That makes more sense to me."

Robert's features softened.

He emptied his cup and gestured for me to come behind the counter. I followed him to the floor-length mirror.

When Robert told me to bare my back, I did.

He asked me to hold still.

I said, "I've been waiting for things to get better or worse, waiting to feel happy or sad, until I woke up one day, and there was nothing to wait for, nothing. What I waited for was passing by me," and I gasped for air. "I went on so stubborn I would've died waiting. You need to have something to leave it behind. But nothing's here for me. I don't have anything, I never lose nothing."

"You know," Robert said, "you can come here whenever." Robert had offered me help with finances before, and I'd refused him. He couldn't expect me to rely on him. But he looked at my belly and acted as if it were not an obstacle, as if it were his own child. "I bought this place for you."

"What if I don't want to come here?"

He laughed. "Koreans love even the terrible parts of people," he said. "We love different."

With the tube, Robert drew on my back.

My eyes roved over the sweeping lines. His fist gripping the lipstick. My bones shook out of some illicit feeling. Uttering a moan, I felt his line stop for a second, then go on. "North and South," he said. "It's an arbitrary line. It's not a natural border. The border is manufactured and maintained. It doesn't actually exist."

When he was done, he cleaned the edges.

Twisting toward the mirror, I let out an unexpected cry.

The drawing took up the whole length of my back. The bright red line started between my shoulders and dropped down my right side, rounding at my hips and buttocks. I looked over my shoulder, looking at the woman who had taken on a sense of dignity.

"It's a tiger," I said.

Robert shook his head. "These are the mountains and plains above, and the inlets and harbors below," he said. "It's Korea."

I choked at the sight of it. "It's beautiful."

"The South doesn't want to rebuild the North. And the North doesn't trust the South," he said. "But all of it used to be one nation. It was a society which shared a culture and a language, and it was ours."

"Then it's a map."

He touched the corner of my chin and drew me closer to the mirror, where I could see my breath. "No, it's a flag."

I couldn't stop staring at the curved lines that made my body shimmer and move. He gazed at me through the mirror.

"Every country has a right to a civil war," he said. "It's not death that I fear but the denial of an end."

After the hour had passed, Robert dressed me again.

For some reason, I didn't want him to cover my back. The shirt pressed against me, and I missed my twin in the mirror; the picture of what could've been facing what must now be possible. I was shaking as I went out the doors. The stain on my lips had been left unbroken.

~

SUNGHO STOOD AT THE top of the stairs, playing with his heavy ring of work keys. He nodded to the smaller rooms. "We'll take one of these."

Huran's voice came from behind him. "The way she talks to me when you're not here."

I told Sungho I wanted to stay on opposite sides since it afforded us privacy. I was explicit about my reasoning, in hopes that he'd understand. This had an effect I didn't expect from Sungho. "It's my choice." He pointed his keys like a teacher in front of a blackboard pointing with a stick. "I want to stay in the smaller room."

"Are you sure?" I asked him.

Huran said I had the gall to argue with him.

Sungho usually didn't ask his mother to stop, but this time he did. He said to me, "You spend all your time with her. You and my mother only have each other. Let her have the room she wants, Insuk. Can't you let it go this one time?"

"Then you and your mother can take the smaller rooms," I snapped. "I'll stay with Henry in the master."

Sungho's expression changed without warning—a trigger pulled and released into the dark. "You don't know enough to be scared of what you say. You say anything. You've made things difficult for me," he said. "Your words plant seeds."

Sungho said every one of my actions bore my signature.

Huran's quiet was the first sign of danger. Huran herself was beaten so often by her husband she must've known.

The lines of the drawing on my back curled and crawled under my shirt. I climbed the steps toward him. "Then you should learn to be a farmer."

Sungho jerked back and, in one movement, tensed his arm and pitched his ring of keys toward me. The keys hit my right hip so hard I thought it had shattered before I hit the ground. Instantly, my hip swelled at the joint, and there was blood.

Huran backed herself into the hallway.

Sungho's face contorted, and he ran toward me.

If it was Korean to love even the terrible parts, and to call these things love, then maybe I was American. Huran said it was my own fault for provoking him. I closed my eyes from the pain on my right side, and when I opened them again, Sungho's and Huran's shadows had left me. The more unbearable my outer life, the more beauty I seemed to notice in my inner life. Like right now, over me was a garden of lilacs bowing from the waist, and if you saw my expression, you wouldn't believe how I could've given up, because nothing could hurt me anymore, and I became the light shining at the center of that garden tended by my mother and my father and the tiger.

THERE WAS AN UGLY bruise down the side of my trunk. Sungho and Huran didn't talk about the risk to the child in my belly—too awful to consider. I was bleeding in a matter of days, but no one wanted to connect the events. Sungho got me a pill used abroad, from somebody at church, to clear the rest of it. I locked myself in the bathroom, laid in the tub. My body thrashed from an invisible lightning, striking my pelvis for hours, my nails gouging the tub, until I pushed out two fistfuls of a gray mass. Huran said we couldn't afford another mouth anyhow, and I agreed with her. When I saw Henry, I felt as if I'd disposed of him, too. Sungho said, "It wasn't like me." Then he ran around in circles and disappeared into the dry cleaners like it was a mousehole.

So I lived in the smaller room facing the street. The sunrise belonged to me, as did the children's feet slap-slapping the pavement. Plum leaves dappled the sidewalk. Moths rested on the window. Light patterned the ceiling like tide pools. Eaves hung low on rainy days. Henry was far across the hallway, and I didn't mind it. At night, I admired the precise right angle of the light from the streetlamp falling over my sill. Crickets chirped louder when the sprinklers came on. I dragged myself as a lump into my sheets. I wanted time to fly like an arrow across my life. The morning after the miscarriage, the first thing Huran told me: "You won't know until you're older, but he's my child. The heart of a mother is impossible to fold."

~

THREE WEEKS LATER, I left the townhome when the dogwood trees turned red, their leaves flame-tipped in the sun, and I marched through the supermarket and into the back room. Buckets of water, pricing guns, and rubber aprons lay across the shelves. The staff noticed me, and not a minute later, Robert appeared in the doorway.

"You don't have to talk. I just want to ask you a couple of questions," Robert said. "Zero is not at all. Three is often."

I nodded.

"Are you in any danger?"

"Two."

He stared at my belly. "Sungho did this to you?"

"Two."

"You regret losing the baby?"

"Two."

"You think about running?"

"Three."

"Will you be safe?"

"Zero."

"Are you scared for Henry?"

"One."

"Do you think about me?"

"Two."

"Did you know I'd come?"

"Three."

"You want my help?"

"Three."

"Do you want me?"

"Three."

I undressed a second time, the air brushing my shoulders and stomach and legs, still shaped roundly from my loss. On the windowsill was a vase filled with nothing but light, as if a neglected plant would flower anyway. Feeling the cold outline of the chair, I told him to trace the borders of the parts usually hidden. This time, everywhere. With a steady hand, he began with my lips.

7

UKISHIMA MARU

Maizuru, 1945

AT EIGHTEEN, ROBERT'S MOTHER TOOK HER father's name, Goil, as her first name after he died so she could ward off Japanese soldiers from knocking on her door on Jeju Island. In occupied Korea of 1943, Goil was soon conscripted for war projects in Ominato in northern Japan. Laboring alongside free Japanese workers, she was dispatched to the air base construction site for dangerous assignments not given to her Japanese counterparts. Housed in a shack for Korean laborers, fifteen feet deep by seven feet wide, as spacious as some toilets, nobody could tell her apart from a man—a skeleton was a skeleton. No basic necessities, the laborers were given less than pigs and cattle; the deprivation caused untold deaths. Koreans caught fleeing during US bombing raids were lynched for fear of an uprising. They assigned Robert's mother a number—five. When she returned home, she wouldn't accept sums of five. If you offered five nuts, she removed one. When counting, she skipped from four to six. She refused to pay any amount ending in five and added another won to escape the number she was called in the field.

If Goil had known the Japanese emperor would announce his surrender in 1945, she might've foreseen the panic that spread throughout Japan. They feared how Koreans would react to liberation. What if they sought vengeance? Took up arms, seizing company tools and sharpened bamboos? How could the Japanese coexist with a freed and sizable Korean population they had put on their own doorsteps? Terror mounted as news came out about cost-saving measures. Companies had no way to compensate the Korean laborers or reimburse their wages deducted on the grounds of cutting costs. Their desperation ought to have been a warning. They ordered Koreans out of Ominato in haste and without protocol. In August, one week after the Japanese surrender at the end of the Second World War, four thousand laborers and their families were put on board the Japanese ship *Ukishima Maru* to return home to the Korean port of Busan.

Goil and a group of other Koreans refused to board the ship before formal repatriation operations got underway.

Goil had suspicions about why the ship was departing ahead of official processes. Moreover, the Japanese crew had chosen a dangerous coastal route over a direct one across open seas. The crew didn't say why they had picked that route over any other. No one could give a reason for the planned detour into Maizuru Harbor. There were reports the crew had been attacked with torpedoes from Allied submarines on the way to Ominato. The crew had only just arrived before being assigned the risky mission to deport Korean laborers and set off so soon into a liberated Korea. In enemy territory, the crew feared being arrested or packed away to forced labor camps. Three of the crew escaped boarding the *Ukishima Maru*, despite the threat of capital punishment. Perhaps the crew never planned to go to Korea.

Many of the laborers taunted Goil. "If you want to stay here, go ahead, but they won't spread your ashes with ours."

They said she'd lost her mind.

Some pitied her. "What's worse than going home to find nobody waiting for you? All the things that gave you courage don't even exist anymore."

The crew forced Goil onto the ship.

Since she kicked and thrashed, they put her in a closet.

The families tried to reason with her: "We're free now," but Goil wouldn't let her guard down.

Two days after departing Ominato, the *Ukishima Maru* detoured into Maizuru Harbor as planned, then suddenly exploded. The blast lifted the ship's hull straight up over the dark lip of water in an inverted V before it plunged down. The cold water found its way through the ship's walls. Goil set her mouth in a grim line and escaped.

The ship was overweight, built to carry eight hundred forty-one passengers. Ten thousand was the high estimate for those killed; five hundred, the low estimate for the number of bodies found right after the explosion. Japanese officials forbade counting the bodies that continued to surface, found hardly human from vascular marbling— their soft tissue a shroud on the seafloor.

Goil survived the explosion. She paddled ashore, and the crew caught her at the docks. They put her in the Maizuru hospital and ordered her to wait.

A metal shard had lodged in her leg. The doctor told her fifty-three stitches. Goil asked for sixty.

The Japanese government ruled that the *Ukishima Maru* had struck an American mine. Goil said the explosion was deliberate. Why had the names of the laborers not been recorded when they boarded? What was the rush to cross into Maizuru? How had only the crew escaped the blast? Goil said the Japanese feared the Koreans would testify against them at war crimes trials or give out information about their base. Any record of those who were on board was gone in postwar burnings. For the sake of empire, damaging files were destroyed. Authorities blocked investigation. Before a search was conducted, the primary evidence, the *Ukishima Maru*, was reduced to scrap metal, a sunken mass glittering like jellyfish at the bottom of the sea.

ROBERT THOUGHT BACK TO when he learned English as a boy on Jeju Island. Robert was four when he was given an alphabet booklet with the exercise: "Draw a ship from the letter *K*."

Trick was you had to lie *K* on its back, so the straight line became the ocean:

You could also use *K* to draw the *Ukishima Maru*:

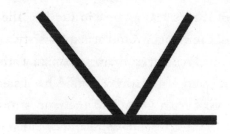

Every *K* stood for two hundred Koreans.

$$K$$

Survivors sent word across Japan: Do not board the ships. Goil didn't give warnings like the others. "They didn't believe me," she told Robert, all those years later. "What was I supposed to do to convince them? They won't listen even if you try to save them." He couldn't tell if there was another reason Goil woke up at night and left her corner of the room and limped out to the island's edge, the moon caught on one side of her face, and stared into the shadowy sea. Goil refused to be a witness. She neither confirmed nor denied that the ship was anchored when the crew debarked before the explosion. Japan's Supreme Court rejected the case brought by survivors. Despite suspicion of explosives on board, the investigation was closed. Goil came back from the explosion as debris. She was floating debris, but she never reached the shore, and there was no sign of her anywhere. What would've been the direct route from Ominato to Busan wrote the first stroke for the character *human*.

~

IN APRIL 1948, three years after the *Ukishima Maru*, Goil was on the sea, dropping her nets into the water, when mainland South Korean police, backed by US troops, landed on Jeju Island's shores in boatloads to slaughter would-be commies and refugees from the North. Goil watched as they chucked slabs of rock to grandfathers and grandsons, told them to stone each other to death. Then both were shot with a resounding end. Bones were scraped off the roads like rice off the bottom of a pot. The Jeju Island governor said sixty thousand had died and forty thousand had fled to Japan. Fires marked the ridgeline, dissolved the night sky. Villagers swirled as ash in the air. Flames reached the horses in the padlocked barns. Goil warned him, "When you're on a sinking ship, don't trust anybody. Don't listen to anybody."

Robert recalled the stitches on Goil's belly from giving birth—a secret door to that inner garden between her and her son. Robert didn't want to think of the dissolution of that door with her death and how he'd spend the rest of his life in search of the road to that door.

Robert was five when he saw a picture of the whole country. If the country had no stitches, it looked like a tiger.

Robert drew the tiger from memory:

The Korean War came two years later in 1950. Goil heard on the radio that it was "a light skirmish" with commies—to be scared off with the threat of atom bombs. In those days, a war could go on for as long as memory; a war among survivors, capable of great brutality. The North and South, like the bull's horns, pointed in different directions. And it was not the atom bomb but napalm, sticky fire, that Americans dropped on villages in the North and bridges in the South, turned into flames. Goil, thinking quickly, coaxed a Busan man to marry her, and she escaped Jeju Island. All she told Robert was that the man was his father, and he died from a stroke in June 1953—one month before the cease-fire.

~

ROBERT, AS A SCHOOLBOY, picked up reading Langston Hughes. The poet mocked Americans for praising the Japanese. Hughes connected subjugation by the Japanese Empire with racial discrimination in the US. Hughes's vision of liberation underscored the legacy of human destruction on the streets of America. The perpetrators and the victims, the diggers of mass graves and those who must lie in them, the collaborators and the sympathizers, the prisoners and the liberators. Robert wanted to see the poet's country for himself. GIs put money in his pocket, and Robert drew them pictures of tigers. He counted the bills with his small fingers: one, two, three, four . . . six.

8

HURAN

San Jose, 1995

HURAN WAS FOND OF WALKING ALONG THE CREEK shaded by overarching trunks and branches and broad-leaves, winding behind the apartments toward the market square. She started the journey without a thought. No groceries were needed, but she wanted to give Insuk space. Sixty now, she felt the tiredness of the mile behind her. No one else was on the path. Hearing the water prattle, she felt relieved. The stream was trickling after weeks without rain. She felt enamored of this walk, though it was nothing more than a dirt path beyond an ivy-covered fence between the town and the freeway. It was unlike her to feel attached to so unkept and hidden a place as this, but her chest pounded with excitement. Settling into a pace, she focused on her heels as they met the ground, the upward swing as the earth pushed her toes up. She was not so much walking as the earth was transporting her. Huran wouldn't call herself agile, yet she could pump her legs along this path.

Huran stilled her strides to look out at the creek. If Insuk or Sungho could see her, they'd say she appeared ages younger. The sparkling, clear water lit up her eyes.

Out of nowhere the base of the tree on the ridge above her snapped loose from the ground. It could've been the sound of lightning. It happened too quickly for her to be startled.

A crackling boom, then the serrated edges of fibrous bark tore into paper strips. Its graceful pendulous branches, acutely angled, slammed their olive-winged crown over the creek. The crown braced against the fence along the freeway and split the whorls of chain-linked metal. The wiry gap exposed the shiny roofs of cars veering to a stop. Through the windshields, faces no bigger than her fingernail.

Huran was standing right under the tree, the trunk only a foot above her head. It was odd how the ground had shifted beneath her. The way it was fluid for a second.

She might have cried, if no one were watching.

A tree had fallen, and she didn't move. The people in the cars shouted to her, but she couldn't hear them.

They asked if she was okay.

Huran went on toward the main road.

They called her again, but she didn't look behind her.

Two fire trucks and three police cars arrived. Drivers and passersby snapped pictures. Huran hurried on the path along the creek and wondered if Insuk worried she'd been gone too long. By now she understood, as Insuk understood, that you could live in the same house as strangers. Then a voice called to her. They waved at her to come back. Fearing she might be stopped, Huran stared at the ground and walked on to the market square.

~

THE WEEK BEFORE EASTER, the church grandmothers took commuter vans to the Milpitas senior center. On the drive, they heard a taped sermon by a young priest from Sacramento who had visited a year ago. They agreed he had long and slender fingers for playing the piano after Eucharist. They commented on the delicate timbre of his voice— Christlike, swaddled in fine tones. The grandmothers often played his tapes. It didn't chafe the ears like their priest in residence, whose coughs escaped him in thrashes. A voice should ring like a bell, not stomp like a shoe.

They gathered in the mess hall. Lined on cafeteria tables were cartons of boiled eggs, watercolors, paintbrushes, pens, sketchbooks, and straw baskets. The grandmothers were competing in the church Easter contest. Groups of seven or eight grandmothers each decorated one basket of eggs to display in the church auditorium on Easter. Churchgoers bought raffle tickets to vote on the best overall basket and runner-up. For years the same grandmothers had won. Their group presented in matching red visors and red vests and red lipstick. The prettiest grandmothers, they had clear and youthful voices and read the week's homily.

Huran thought the grandmothers put too much of themselves into the reading. You ought to read the homily as a distant observer. They clothed their words, stretching the delicate fibers of meaning like stockings; if only she had the words to steer them away from their mistakes. But she felt embarrassed to make a correction. They sang the loudest and each year boasted a basket of eggs that won the majority of the votes.

This year Huran was determined to win. But she was shocked to see thistle-shaped laces, crystalline designs, cobalt-blue-and-white chinoiserie, golden foil carvings, dandelion foliage, circling miniature trains, waltzing clay figures, music boxes in nests. She felt overwhelmed by sketches of eggs wrapped in colorful yarn and sewn-on flowers. Copper-charred shells for a burning bush. Sculpted ice palaces of velvet-lined eggs. She couldn't comprehend eggs in sandglasses, impossibly slipped through a narrow hollow.

A grandmother pinched her. "What're you working on, Huran?"

"I don't see any sketches for your group," said Yonju, the team leader for the red group. "You must be hiding them from us."

Huran hadn't had time to make any but couldn't say. "Don't worry." Huran tapped her head. "It's all up here."

The grandmothers gasped.

"You still do things from memory?" Yonju slapped Huran's arm playfully. "What a remarkable thing. We're all ready to die tomorrow but you."

Huran felt more at ease with Insuk than she did with the grandmothers, who complimented her needlessly.

Yonju said, "If my son had stopped chasing after new jobs in Silicon Valley, I'd have a room to myself on the top floor like you." Yonju thumbed her rosary beads, like dry beans on a fishing line. "Judas himself would crawl back from that place with his tail between his legs. He was an original member of the first start-up in the world!"

Huran tried to save face. "Your son and daughter-in-law are innocent and gentle," she reassured Yonju. "Insuk is stubborn."

"She's probably terrified of you."

"Terrified, of me?"

"Watch out," Yonju said. "A cornered rat will bite a cat!"

A hoot came from the grandmothers.

One sharpened her tongue at Huran. "You only had one son. I bet you torture her like a prison guard."

Another said to her, "It's not popular to be mean to your daughter-in-law anymore."

"Poor Insuk's on her own like me." Yonju opened a carton and sized the eggs. "No matter how my son and my daughter-in-law try to convince me, I'm going to be buried in Korea. But the grave rental is egregious. I'll be paying rent for the rest of my death."

"Caskets are expensive, like cars," Huran said.

"Just bury me raw—straight in the ground," and Yonju laughed. "Soon as we're gone, our sons won't give us another thought. Our graves are at the mercy of their wives, our daughters-in-law."

Huran dropped her egg on the floor.

"First one's a winner." Yonju cracked it on the table and gave Huran the crunchy egg. "You get to eat before any of us."

A grandmother said to Yonju, "Oh my God. It's like that accident."

Yonju nodded. "The Sampoong Department Store collapse," she said. "It's all over the Korean news."

The grandmothers joined in. "Oh my God, it's awful."

"You didn't hear about it?" Yonju asked Huran. "Hundreds of people died." Yonju leaned across the cafeteria table. "Here's the thing," she said. "The owner of the building was seen fleeing the site before it collapsed. But he abandoned the building without telling his own daughter-in-law, who worked on the floor!"

"So he killed his daughter-in-law?" Huran asked.

"Who cares if she lived, at this point. Would you ever want to go home again?" Yonju said. "I'd get rid of my husband first. An in-law without a husband is just a stranger."

When Huran picked up another egg, it slipped from her.

"Stop your antics," Yonju said. "You're just hungry, aren't you?"

Huran's group looked at her. She blinked to keep her eyes from looking so wrung out. Then she slowly reached for another egg. "Can we talk about something else?"

"Don't get angry, Huran. You have no one but us," Yonju said. "I'd rather risk it with the serial killers in this country than with the buildings in ours!"

The grandmothers burst into laughter again.

These days, Huran dreamed a pill bug came out of her ear to play on her chest. She opened her eyes and heard footsteps in her ear tunnel. The pill bug could be a thought that had slipped from her mind and was struggling to get back in, or it could be someone who had died and couldn't afford a proper grave site. Huran recited the Prayer for Souls in Purgatory—she could avoid trouble by praying sincerely. But why would they come back as a pill bug for a burial—was her ear a tomb with no rental?

~

ON EASTER, Huran ditched Communion and went to the auditorium, where she bought a raffle ticket and strolled the rows of tables on which the egg basket entries were displayed. Huran stepped lightly in a pink hanbok with rose ties and cream moccasins. It was scandalous to scope the tables before the closing blessings and before the other grandmothers had arrived.

Huran was eager to try the fancy eggs. The contest rules required baskets to be the same willow weave with braided handle arches. Every basket had to carry three hundred eggs or less. White placards on the tables listed the groups of grandmothers. Looking at the placards, Huran stopped at her own basket.

Insuk appeared in the hallway alone. She walked toward Huran in a purple hanbok, sheer muslin fabric over a modest top and skirt. Seeing Insuk's hair in soft waves and her gently arched brows that opened her face, Huran recalled how Insuk had been just a child in her late mother's green hanbok on her wedding night.

Insuk studied Huran's group basket. "Three hundred blank eggs."

It was more than Huran had expected her to say. Huran said carefully, "The basket is the way it came. The eggs too. Except for one egg in the center."

Insuk read her neat handwriting: *Mea culpa.*

"It took me a long time to write it."

"It's not like killing chickens anymore."

Huran chuckled. "But I can still fight a driving instructor. She ran for the hills."

Other grandmothers filed into the auditorium. The grandmothers in red visors and red vests and red lipstick banded together. They formed a primal crossing in a V-shape. Their arms locked together—dark spots on their skin like a pack of dalmatians.

Yonju ripped her rice cake, offered a bite to Insuk, who opened her mouth and gnawed on it. "These days, your top and skirt should be different colors, Insuk. They're not supposed to match."

"Yonju," Huran teased, "you're as red as a dog's dick."

The other grandmothers stared at Huran as if something within them had been illuminated.

"You're acting different today," Yonju said.

Huran was hoping for a reaction from Insuk and was hurt by her expressionless face, though it was petty for Huran to notice it.

"You showed up with quite the basket," Yonju said. "We were worried because you dropped half your eggs. We're too old to even drop eggs anymore!"

The grandmothers bellowed.

Huran shrugged. "I was a little shaken up at the time," she said. "A tree fell right on top of me."

Insuk cocked her head. "When did this happen?"

"On my walk to the market."

Yonju said to Insuk, "Don't pity the old hag. Huran keeps you under her thumb because you're a good daughter-in-law." Yonju chewed her rice cake. "You're only letting Huran boast by being kind to her in front of us. She's a dull knife, you know."

Huran, startled by Yonju's words, headed to the tables for the announcements. No one followed her.

The priest in residence stood at the front of the auditorium. In his hoarse voice, he named the winning basket.

Yonju's group had won as usual, for crystallizing the delicate eggshells. Their group cheered, jumping up and down, careful about the skirts under their vests.

The runner-up was Huran's basket, lauded for its simplicity.

Huran beamed at her group. She noticed Insuk reach for an egg to crack on the table.

After the luncheon of eggs from all the basket entries, emptied over hours, dipped in soy sauce or salt, Huran and Insuk met Sungho and Henry in the parking lot. Insuk said she couldn't understand why Huran kept coming back when the grandmothers were so mean to her. "Our meanness is our kindness," Huran said. "It's how we stay close. If they only had nice things to say, it'd be hard to trust them." Lingering, Huran glanced behind her. The building had none of the usual signs of a Catholic church, the arches or high spires or golden crosses. It was just a warehouse with a slanted roof, white lettering. You could be driving by, and if you weren't paying attention, you'd miss the sharp turn into the parking lot. From the outside, it would be clear to any observer that Huran loved these people for how they couldn't be mistaken for anyone but themselves. For anyone seeing them now, let them know she was among her peers. Let them see the lives at the heart of this city as the whole of the universe. Let them face Easter with a sense of knowing such a place existed for them. Huran's vision blurred and then came in bright and distinct.

~

ON NEW YEAR'S DAY, Huran found herself in the hospital. It was thanks to a man called Robert that the doctor had found a slot in his schedule for them, and no one seemed to suspect it was anything more than a favor. The doctor said Huran had had two strokes between Easter and New Year's. She was lucky Insuk had heard a thud in the night and brought her to the emergency room. Sungho left the hospital to check on Henry, who was often wandering the valleys with a pen and notepad. Insuk stayed behind in the room with Huran.

Huran said to Insuk, "I don't know my real birthday. My parents thought I'd die as a baby."

Yonju had passed after Easter. Huran said at their age, nothing was unexpected. She'd known it was coming by how Yonju spoke without remorse.

Insuk rubbed Huran's hands and massaged her ears. She touched Huran at the hospital more than she ever had. She wouldn't do these things at home. It seemed Insuk couldn't stop herself, and Huran couldn't refuse. "Your ears are stiff," Insuk said. "They should be soft, so your insides can be soft."

"If I had soft ears, I'd believe everything I hear."

Insuk said Henry had soft ears.

"Henry reminds me of Sungho's father," Huran said. "It's hard to know what he's thinking."

Huran and Insuk could unite as parents complaining about their children.

"Funny thing is," Huran added, "I worry about you more than Sungho."

Insuk chuckled this time. "It's hard to hate someone for so long," she said. "It's a real commitment. Maybe your feelings started to swing the other way."

"I didn't hate you," Huran said. "I needed you."

"Oh, I know I hated you."

"Ah," she said. "You started it."

"I guess that kitchen on my wedding night was pretty cold," and they both grinned, looking at each other.

As Huran spoke, Insuk worked her thumbs into Huran's stiff palms. "Babies like me stuck around for the occupation," Huran said, "and yours didn't even get to see a McDonald's."

Insuk paused, then asked about the egg basket.

"When I first saw it," Insuk said, "I thought, what kind of person thinks of something like this? Three hundred eggs, unpainted and untouched. But one egg in the middle with the words *Mea culpa*."

Many grandmothers couldn't draw by hand because of an inner trembling, but Huran had gone through the basket's volume of eggs to paint every letter.

Huran could tell Insuk was focused on her.

"I understood those words," Insuk said. "The priest called your basket profound. He said it was the perspective of God looking at us. Every one of us a perfect egg. But the priest was wrong. You made it for me. You wanted me to see, and it was everything you've wanted to say to me. For all those years we couldn't get along." Insuk took a shaky breath. "All those years you were awful to me."

Huran lay still in her bed.

"I don't have any bad feelings toward you," Insuk said. "Not because I don't think you deserve them. But because I'm tired of carrying them around. I was thinking about those words on that egg. *Mea culpa*. And I was thinking you were sorry about one thing more than anything else. You were saying those words to me, and you were saying them for the baby I couldn't have. Suppose the baby lived on. Suppose they're waiting for you right now. Would you be a better grandmother to them in the afterlife?"

Huran raised her head, nodding, up and down, and her tears broke through after years of putting them behind her. Insuk wiped Huran's face and fixed her hair.

Suppose it was just Huran and Insuk, and Sungho had left them alone. Suppose Huran and Insuk had sold the hanbok and bought the farm and spent the days killing chickens in their aprons and the nights curling into each other's arms by the stove. Huran understood it'd always been them, together. Outside the window, a faint swollen light. An invisible boot snuffed out the sun. Huran spent the night holding on to Insuk. Suppose Huran met her in another life, and they lived as sisters. Though this room they shared was not her first choice, it was the first room Huran and Insuk had entered together.

~

HURAN WAS DEAD, but she wasn't a ghost. Just had her eye on things.

Her funeral couldn't be over with quickly enough. Months passed before Insuk cleaned out Huran's room. Insuk put Huran's blankets in the closet. She donated

Huran's scarves, clothes, and shoes. Insuk kept the hospital throw in the bottommost drawer of her dresser with her mother's green hanbok.

When Huran was alive, Insuk had cleaned efficiently, but now it took her the whole day to pack things away.

Insuk opened and closed the fridge. Insuk seemed to decide to walk to the market square.

Insuk chose the path along the creek.

Huran watched her follow the path until she stopped at the vacant space of the tree. Insuk looked closer at the magnitude and width of the broken branches swept aside, leaving a terrifying void. Insuk appeared overwhelmed to see the wreck and imagine such a tree breaking from the ground in an explosion. It was true—it was a mighty tree. Huran and Insuk were transfixed by its absence. Perhaps Insuk had stopped because she couldn't spare herself the guilt of not having given it a thought before. Perhaps Insuk shared Huran's sense of foolishness for losing the woman whom she had lived with so closely. It was this woman Huran wanted to tell her feelings to now. It was her thoughts Huran wanted to hear. Huran turned, as Insuk turned, onto the path, and the breeze hooked them in the same shadow.

9

SUNGHO

San Jose, 1997

THE LARGE EIGHT BALL STOOD OUT TO SUNGHO AS
he approached the entrance of the pool hall where Mansae
had gathered local businesses. Sungho paused to consider
the black vinyl sign—its round shape stopped the light from
entering the hall. It was one eye meeting his two as Sungho
came through the doors. Still wearing his work shirt from
the cleaners, Sungho stepped onto the green-and-yellow
carpet as if he were passing over piles of leaves on his way to
the main floor. The pool tables had been pushed against the
wall to make space. There was the feeling of the distant past
in the dark hall with bronze fixtures. Fifty or more men

in collared shirts talked while jingling their keys. Busying their hands was all they could do to keep still.

Sungho hadn't noticed the platform at the rear.

On the platform stood Robert, facing the doors. Above him was a banner with the words *Liberation Shinmun*.

Sungho didn't know why, but he stared back at the vinyl sign, which now appeared as a black hole.

Robert addressed the room. "We're paranoid. We can't shake off the madness of suspecting our own people."

Sungho hadn't noticed before the way the eight ball cast a shadow almost like wings. Robert looked slender and straight—gray suit under a black coat. His subtle and slow movements put the men who watched him at ease.

Robert's voice filled the hall. "Mass bankruptcy. Banks gutted." He described the IMF crisis, looking out over their wordless, inscrutable faces. "You can't assume employment among companies, friendship among friends, and family among family."

No one took their eyes off him.

It was harder to tell where the door was, whether it was behind or in front of them, whether it was the eight ball or Robert that sucked them in.

More men arrived—their footsteps skirted Sungho.

Robert laughed grimly. "I started *Liberation Shinmun* because you have to convince people to liberate them-selves," he said. "And we can liberate others because we've already liberated ourselves."

Robert stepped off the platform, and he placed his hand over the breast pocket of his coat. "Here are the pages I've written for every *Shinmun* issue," he said. "Tonight, I ask for your support of my life's work."

The room divided into groups by the eight ball and in the rear where Robert stood.

One man said, "You say free North Koreans. You're digging into hard ground."

Another added, "You're putting us in danger. The *Shinmun* should be illegal."

It seemed to Sungho that Robert was evangelical about a whole and united Korea. If Robert planned to use his words to change the minds of men, it didn't seem that he'd considered anything beyond that. He wanted apologies from the US and the Korean governments, damages from Japan, and a record of those killed and imprisoned since the colonial period, which seemed as unrealistic as joining the Koreas. In all likelihood, his writings and speeches, in which he once presented himself as a peaceable man, now revealed him to be a dangerous one.

"What is up or down depends on where you live," Robert said. "We stand against oppression on both sides of the border between North and South. We must be the ones to free her."

The groups shuffled like herds of animals. The groups near Robert grew. There were two or three men in the front, where Sungho stood, who walked out of the hall.

Robert nodded toward the doors, through which his words picked their way along the El Camino strip to the restaurant, the supermarket, the video rental shop, the karaoke bar where people worshipped after church, the bakery where their wives and mothers tangoed with bread tongs. To Mountain View and its technology companies, harvesting children from San Jose, Cupertino, Sunnyvale, Milpitas, and Fremont—children tramping off their migration in the classrooms, as redeemers of restaurant workers and liquor store clerks and massage parlor employees, children of obsidian hair and nervous tics who raced off to San Francisco. To Dumbarton Bridge toward enclaves of sprawling retirement homes for their older selves. Homes with windows vast enough to plague their sleep with the East Bay view.

"Post-liberation, my mother returned to Busan," Robert said, "but she was deprived of the feeling of home. It wasn't the same country she'd been forced to leave. It wasn't the one that gave her the strength to live until she could see it again."

Robert had a conciliatory air about him as he peered over them. The men pushed farther to the rear.

Robert asked the remaining men to consider these words. "What we commit to forgetting we also commit to memory."

"Reunification is a load of crap," a voice said.

Then a second added, "Say North and South are good with the plan and open the border. US troops would get moved way up to the North. China and Russia won't have the US on their doorsteps."

Robert stepped up onto the platform again and raised his head so they could see him. "If China or Russia showed any aggression, it would end badly for them. We're nearing the turn of the century. Wars are also fought with economic and political pressures."

"The North depends on powerful allies," a third said. "They're doing what China wants. They won't align themselves with Japan—on principle. You can add the fact that the North has yet to meet the universal standard of human rights."

Robert said, "Reunification can be a structure of one country, two systems."

Sungho opened his mouth. "Reunification is shy two trillion dollars." Sungho was suddenly conscious of the men staring at him.

"Sungho." Robert's eyes settled on him. "East and West Germany had a two-system infrastructure. The North will need help, but the North has resources. Combine that with the South—"

"What the South used to be," Sungho said. "The price isn't worth the yield if your belly button is bigger than your stomach."

This got a laugh out of the men.

Sungho's words appeared to split the room in half. Two large groups formed, and one rallied behind Sungho. He was standing between Robert and the eight ball.

Robert smiled at the floor. "You're a faithful man," he said. "I believe we can correct our mistakes. Do it all over again. Why is it hard to accept that a place like the North exists?"

Sungho said, "I don't want any part of it."

"But it is a part of you," he said. "Even the horrible parts."

Robert was right—the war was within. It was natural to want to fight but senseless to try and justify a reason. Sungho recalled the smoking hills, a sharp white bone in the dirt. All to call themselves Korean. Inside the eight ball, they couldn't fool anyone but themselves. "Reunification is appealing," Sungho said. "We're all victims." Sungho wanted to know why Robert stood above them. What about Robert let him speak for Sungho, when Sungho didn't ask him to do so. "But victims silence victims."

Robert argued the surest bet for a united Korea was two provinces with a central authority. The US was unreliable. Russia, aggressive. Japan, authoritarian. China ignored their own problems. The South was unstable, making an opening. A united Korea was no threat to democracy. When asked about the probability of corporations in the South abusing cheap labor in the North, Robert said it couldn't be avoided. He was talking hard losses—people would die. There would be radio apologies, printed apologies, and televised apologies.

Robert said, "The DMZ is an active war zone—a border created by US and Soviet forces after the occupation. Like the Berlin Wall that divided East and West Germany. After the wall came down, Koreans everywhere felt optimistic. Reunification was possible again."

The men opened a path for Robert to reach Sungho.

Robert said to him, "I always assumed there was a wall without seeing it for myself. But when I saw the footage on the news, I realized the wall was never there to begin with. There was never a wall."

Sungho headed for the door, but an arm stopped him.

"You're quite engaging." Robert released him. "I didn't expect it from you. I'm glad you shared your opinions tonight."

Sungho and Robert were two oceans crosshatching over each other, each mistaking the opposing current for the wake of his own.

"Why are you living in the past? Why drag us through the wreckage?" Sungho said. "Why sit down to count losses now—didn't you have enough? I don't need to lose more than I already have, and I can be proud of the losses I've suffered."

"You're so old-fashioned, Sungho."

Sungho was unnerved by Robert's way of speaking to him. Robert was familiar with Sungho but they hardly ran into each other. Robert looked like he could snap a neck with the force of a trap door but spoke as if he'd read the national library. Robert was not an intellectual or mad with violence. He was not somebody who never caused damage. He did not have political aims. He did not despise people. He did not object to his opposers, but Robert would throw his life away for nothing.

Sungho saw the eight ball and the darkest part of the curve where the light shone most clearly. "Old-fashioned," Sungho said, rolling the word over his tongue, and it put him in mind again of that night on the riverbank where he'd been with Insuk, their tightly coiled bodies years ago. Sungho hadn't suspected him before, but now confirmed what Robert had been hiding from him— what Robert and Insuk had both been hiding—inside the eight ball looking at Sungho. "Who told you that I'm old-fashioned?"

~

THAT SAME NIGHT, Sungho took out a loan from Mansae, under the table, to open his own cleaners in Irvington, in a building where green bottle flies as smooth as sea glass swarmed. Unlatching the door to what until recently had been the storage space for a brownstone coffeehouse, before that a crematorium with high chimneys, Sungho swiped cobwebs from the beams. Under the window was an opossum carcass packed with larvae. Sungho scalpeled the ooze off the floor, disposed of it. He carried in a discarded table but couldn't decide where to put it. Sungho opened the window; the cold air shook him loose. He thought Insuk would love the storage room and the drying machines. "You know one month is a lifetime," Insuk had teased him, along the river. Sungho's hands leaped in front of his face as if to catch himself in a fall. When her father had disappeared, Sungho should've said something then. If Sungho were to count the months he'd spoken to his wife since their marriage, they would add up to zero. Sungho placed the table in the center—the rays of sunlight moored it to the ground. Sungho remembered Insuk telling him to live east of where he worked so that in either direction he wouldn't walk directly into the sun.

SUNGHO RETURNED HOME WITH pictures to show Insuk. He had captured angles of the space. The opened window, the cleaned floors. It was a reel composed of nooks and slants, but each shot was illuminated by a wide beam of light. Insuk looked surprised that Sungho would quit his job and start over again. Sungho told her something he had noticed but never said to her before. "Henry looks just like your father, doesn't he? Do you think your father would be pleased?" These questions must've startled her. Insuk took his hand, and her words led him with deliberate footsteps over soft ground back to the riverbank. "Henry acts more like your father, right?" she said. "I think he has the best parts of us both."

Almost like a bird, she came into his arms without ever opening her wings. The autumn sky was on its last legs. He watched their son go to bed. Sungho lay on the floor next to Insuk, his heart tumbling as if it were washing in the water, holding his breath, and exhaling, stroking the inside of her wrists, her thin arms stretched across his chest, both of them trembling, her eyes bright as she sighed and craned her neck toward him. They must've been ready to love each other again, though it had taken Sungho a decade to lean as close to her as he had once seen in a painting of a garden. There was a prairie, its grass leaning, its stalks brushed by the wind, the barely threaded clouds, and the smell of damp earth.

III

COLONY OF LIGHT

2000–2001

10

HENRY

San Jose, 2000

BY AGE SEVENTEEN, I COULD READ THE VALLEYS after school. I asked of a paw print—who? The glow in the distance—where? And the broken cobweb—when? Light passed through the wings of a moth onto my palm. I tracked soft impressions in the tall grass until I came to the resolution of a chase—a den. Dogs came over the hill, puffing from their run. As I mapped the town, my senses lifted off the ground. From a bird's-eye view, I had no feeling of a separation. The moment life showed itself in the brush, I held still above the earth's roots. Though I came and went, from the townhome to the school to the valleys, I didn't go missing. I could be found as soon as you looked for me. I'd come to you even if you couldn't follow me, and I didn't worry anybody.

These June days, marked by an apocalypse that never came, my face whiskered and my hair tucked behind my ears. I could read my mother and father, who slipped into their bedroom and impressed me for the first time with their laughter. With my grandmother gone, they became harmless like clear soup. Most days, my mother looked for my father, whose face curled tightly with excitement at the sound of her voice. My father drew her out of her dark moods in such a way that I could see her as a girl lying awake at night, a shadow on her cheek, rolling the late hours between her palms into the ball of morning. Then without warning, my parents disappeared into their room, nodding like horses.

I could read Robert at the pool hall, who walked to and from the rear as if painting lines with the bottoms of his shoes. Every time Robert heard footsteps at the door, he raised his head. When he noticed me, he looked as if he'd ask me a question but said nothing. Robert dissolved his businesses and devoted himself to the hall, where men assembled in falling numbers since the crash and the layoffs. He invited activists, city council members, company presidents, but his words didn't travel farther than the pool cue chalk. Only a decade ago, Robert had men and women vibrating at his ears. He couldn't give up, so he hired a young woman to transcribe his writings. The young woman made a clear impression on me: her heart-shaped face with wide, dark eyes and perfect teeth. She seemed to watch me closely when I walked up, opening the door like a trap.

~

IT WAS SUNDAY AFTERNOON—still summer. The sun split my onion skin. I biked in the opposite direction of the townhome—I had no plan. Any creature leaves ripples in its wake, so I followed a metallic taste in the air. I was cutting through the Ohlone College campus, sandbox-square buildings on foothills with red signs and green arrows, when I spotted the young woman from the pool hall. She was slogging a poster across the quad. The young woman was a college student, but it hadn't occurred to me until I saw her on campus. She propped the poster against a skinny tree on a square of earth in the cement. And stood in front of it with her arms out, as if she had put herself on a coatrack, a cross, as if she were jumping out of a plane.

The poster read:

I AM NORTH KOREAN

FREE HUGS!

A child paused at the sign. "Are you North Korean?"

"I am," the young woman said.

The child ran to his mother. His mother said it was an act, a performance. They pondered the sign from the edge of the quad.

The young woman raised her arms higher. People stopped to read but wouldn't get close. I watched from the basketball court. The bell rang between summer classes.

One professor halted in front of her. The professor had on a sweater over a modest skirt. "When's the last time you ate?"

The young woman said nothing.

"You don't stay overnight on campus, do you?"

She dropped her arms. "I don't live at the school if that's what you mean."

The professor pushed cash on her. "You're saying you won't get touched as a North Korean? What's your point?"

The young woman's name was Jennie. Her English was excellent. So were her Chinese and Korean. Her colloquial English came from being a caregiver to elderly Americans before working at the pool hall. "Beijing was shipping defectors back to North Korea. I was eight when I had to escape China," she said. "We fled to Mongolia. Rumor was Mongolia traded with South Korea—people for trees."

"People for trees?" The professor said it was a lie.

"Mongolia needs trees because of its deserts."

"They got trees for you?"

Jennie frowned. "It's a fair trade. Americans will need trees soon. I'm an eighteen-year-old tree," she said. "It's strange how you Americans worship your politicians. The way you buy political merchandise and wear it, like sports teams."

The professor smiled wryly. "If you're a defector, don't they put you in an Ivy League? Don't tell me you're a slacker."

"I applied for Ohlone while I was sleeping in libraries," Jennie said. "I was homeless since no one hires defectors in the South. But I've made it to the same place as you."

The professor said Jennie was lucky to be here.

Jennie said she dreamed of becoming a high-tech assembly line worker, fired for complaining about respiratory illnesses.

"How many trees they give for you?"

Jennie said the professor's joke was expected. Americans felt uneasy about death and suffering. But the economics of capitalism were the same as death—the value of human life.

"It's not how many trees," Jennie said. "It's what kind."

"Ah, psychology." The professor cracked a smile. "You go on sprouting, then."

When the professor left, so did the mother and child.

Jennie fixed her poster and raised her arms.

I couldn't help myself. Tossing my bike onto the court, I crossed the quad in a few strides and fell straight into her arms.

We stood embracing. To my surprise, she didn't feel tense at all. "You." Her tone was relaxed. "You're Henry, right?"

"You can't have your sign up for hugs and stand here alone," I said. "People will think something is wrong. The professor was taking over your sign."

"So you're righteous."

"If you think so," I said. "People need to see what they're supposed to do. We're like animals."

"Then you're reckless."

Few approached the quad.

"I've never been reckless." I told her to watch what happened around us. "No one crosses into something that looks dangerous. They feel accused by you. They'll only come for something they want for themselves."

Just then, another bell rang, and a group of ten or so others walked around us. Some stopped to observe us.

"A crucifix feeds on the past," and I lowered my arms without letting her go. "What you need is a different sign."

"I see," Jennie said. "The desire to be rebellious fades with the desire to belong."

Five, six, then seven joined, holding our shoulders.

I pointed across the quad at the professor, who had stopped to watch us. "The hug isn't for you," I said. "It's for her—it's for us."

Jennie took in the forming crowd. "Why'd you come here?" she said. "I'm not on your side."

Twenty or thirty others corralled around us. Bunched shoulder to shoulder with their arms hanging over each other.

"I thought that was the point," I said. "That we're not on the same side."

"What a surprise," Jennie said.

Hundreds of students gathered that day on the quad. They came from the basketball court and the classrooms and the library. Jennie said it was like when she'd first arrived in Incheon. Standing under the recessed lights of the empty baggage claim, before the government stopped housing her, before her bosses accused her of stealing and grilled her about Northern girls with round faces and red lips, before the Seoul hell where her skin was no longer dusted with powder off the mountains but with ash off the cigarettes, she'd recognized a flash of humanity in a billboard sign. Two figures stood in the center—soft, persistent focus. Shadows crisped the edges. Scratches lightened the grain. No weather, no grass. You might have believed that even the most intractable conflicts could be resolved. The picture of lovers looked unbearably light, as if it weighed nothing at all.

~

HORRIBLE THINGS WERE USUALLY preventable. They transgressed moral and rational boundaries. Otherwise they were terrible. Like a terrible earthquake, a landslide. God's mud. On a weekend night at the pool hall, Jennie counted the register, moving her lips without a sound. Robert disappeared for days at a time. When I asked her about it, she rolled the bills under the tray. "Robert's running out of money, and he's losing friends. Now his customers are younger—recent grads without jobs. The irony is that his dream to unify people has isolated him. There's a reason we haven't unified in fifty years. But he's obsessed with some kind of plan."

Jennie's hands pushed through her jacket sleeves. I asked why she worked for him, and she said, "Only Robert would hire me. I can work until the whole strip is bought up by developers and turned into an office complex." We stepped through the doors and out into the ordinary world. Jennie padded the rear rack of my bike with Robert's writings—precious thoughts he'd put on paper—and sat on them. It seemed as though one must live one's thoughts, or they'd become merely a cushion. She dangled her feet so they wouldn't catch the spokes or my pedaling heels.

Pointing, she directed me twenty miles down a path along Stevens Creek Trail to a lagoon.

Jennie said, "Robert's forty-five now. He's planning to go to Korea by himself. But it's dangerous—he's been too loud about his ideas."

I rode around a pothole. "So you'd heard of him before you started working at the pool hall?"

"Who hasn't heard of Robert?" She played with my loose hair. "Robert talks about an auditorium near the Port of Busan. He's probably going to head there."

We passed through a tunnel. Popped out under the trees. "You're not one of his lackeys, are you?" she asked.

Riding into the tailwind, we picked up speed.

"I've watched him since I was five. Robert gave me a dog and saved his life," I said. "Robert listens to Journey. His favorite song is 'Don't Stop Believin'.' He wants coexistence. He's just an exile who wants to be loved by the country that exiled him."

Then a bird flew into my periphery, and I thought of paws pressing on my collarbones, a wet leathery snout resting on my chest—so that bird I just saw had to be Toto.

"Robert's favorite movies happen to be the same as Kim Jong Il's—the James Bond films. He plays them in the pool hall all the time." The wind picked up, she leaned closer. "They order the same drinks, drive the same cars."

"Who doesn't like those movies?" I said. "You think they're worse than *Titanic*?"

"Koreans love *Titanic*. Because it's so Korean."

I slowed my wheels on a merge.

"People with high moral authority are dangerous," Jennie said into my ear, her words like silk spilling out of a magician's hat. "Their egos depend on their ability to see themselves as moral, so they become dictators just as quickly as they become leaders."

~

IT WAS DARK AT the lagoon. Jennie could see and hopped over the plastic mesh fences. Stiff grass stopped at the bar of white sand. I heard of the salt flats and boat launches but not this place. The wind blew through the trees, whose branches moved as if underwater. The cold water came up to my ankles and split in two. The sound of wings splashing in the lagoon. Swings, with no one in them, going back and forth in the playground. Behind me, mountain ridge knuckles gripped broad, flat valleys. The fronds minted the air. Scalloped skies appeared through the understory. The stars were like holes in a vast gray tarp. The last clouds wagged their tails as they broke off.

Jennie picked up her sandals by the strings, and her bare feet rolled with the dips in the beach.

We tossed our clothes, waded into the water.

The water came waist-high at the buoy. The silver surface rippled, shining into the back of my eyes.

The signs warned, *No lifeguards on duty.*

Jennie reached me at the buoy. Under her arm, she had Robert's papers.

When she crossed my sight on the horizon, I drew out a page of Robert's life. "If Robert wanted to hurt somebody, it'd be different. If he believed he could hurt anybody, he would've done it already." Robert often kept an eye on his watch, and I couldn't tell whether he wanted time to go slower or faster—or whether it was time that wouldn't let go of him. "If he shared his ideas and found out he was wrong, he'd apologize."

Then she tossed Robert's papers into the air, page by page, as if hundreds of insects tore out of their pale molts—blowing away in the wind. Jennie had no qualms as the sheets landed on their backs and floated in circles around us.

"Why'd you do that?" My voice pitched forward as if to catch the thin sheets.

"Robert's a corrupt guy, and Korea has one of the most corrupt systems in the world. The human rights groups endanger the people they're meant to protect, risking the lives of defectors to get support funds from countries like the US, who want to further their own image of moral leadership," she said. "Networks pay celebrity defectors, protected by the state, to demonize North Koreans. A chosen percentage speak on behalf of North Koreans everywhere." Jennie shivered in the swell. "Reunite the country to free North Korea? Who says? The human rights groups that smuggle USB drives into the North and trigger their authorities to execute families? Human rights issues are corrupt. All of it is supposed to fail. Without captivity, there is no liberation."

She stood straight as if her words caught the bottom of the lagoon.

"Don't be stupid, Henry. You don't know about defector suicides in the South. Judicial officers won't report them as what they really are—murders. Defector deaths pile up as paperwork in Seoul's main office, boring public servants, and only once in a while surprising the public. The North never had a monopoly on North Korean deaths."

Time was horrible until it stopped, then it became terrible. My mother's bottommost drawer was horrible until it was filled—her singed uniform, a hospital throw, and two hanboks that didn't fit her—then it became terrible. It was horrible that as my mother and father aged, they missed their own parents. It was terrible that everyone became an orphan eventually. Horrible that my parents would lose half their memories if they ever split up. Terrible that they stayed together for what they hoped to remember. The Robert I knew couldn't be horrible, but if he were to leave us now, he might become terrible. The way an iceberg at sea was terrible. The thing about the lifeboats onboard was horrible. But a sinking ship was always terrible.

Jennie hooted with laughter. "But whatever, right?" She kicked the water, making the papers float away.

Jennie waded closer and told me it was remarkable what I didn't know—yet it was this very part of me she was drawn to because it remained untouched. The water nudged my spine left and right, and I let my arms rise up, inching toward her. She was suspended in the water, leaning slightly back. I dug my feet into the sand, my heels anchoring me. Scooping the water, she kept herself in place. The moon reflecting off the sand below illuminated her in the dark. The light turned us translucent—into the color of the water. I saw the upward curve of her spine, the brushstroke of her thighs. The water dried on our shoulders. I looked down at the elaborate braid of our bodies, and we began to move. We rocked together, rolling with the drag.

~

BY MORNING THE PAPERS had disappeared. Jennie wouldn't ask me about them. I'd picked them up and strung them on my bike as if drying them out on a line, and I rode home with them. Sheets of ink-stained paper flapped around me, trying their wings in the headwind as I pedaled. One page hanging from my handlebar I could still read through its broken ink. I recognized it as Robert's credo—a poster sign he stood up over the earth:

Fratricide is, by definition of the shared human condition, sui-cide. Every human on the planet has a responsibility, one that deserves reflection and careful action, to the reunification of the Koreas and ultimately to ourselves.

On the way back, I stopped by the pool hall. I placed the sheets of paper under the front door. I set the pages there, some dog-eared, with tails tucked between their words, needing rest before being read and taken into any-one's arms. The words met you with their paws raised in the air, their wet dog eyes glinting in the dark, smelling of the early summer rain. I hoped what was written in these pages would be with Robert for what lay ahead of him. I took one last look at the pool hall and hoped Robert wouldn't feel so lost and understood that he belonged any-where his feet could take him because his words together, on these pages, made a wailing sound as ancient and as familiar as the sea.

II

INSUK

Tacoma, 2000

FOUR YEARS AGO, AFTER HURAN'S FUNERAL, Sungho chatted me up after work with conversation he usually saved for his mother. Sungho must've been curious about how we could've grown apart. I could see that Sungho had been a bird caught in a trap all these years and, struggling wildly, had broken his own wings. It wasn't long after Huran passed that Sungho and I were able to meet as if for the second time. I thought of what he had wanted from his mother and mirrored the ways she consoled him. I prepared misugaru shakes in the mornings and herbal soups in the evenings. Pressed the point between his thumb and index finger for headaches. Filled a bath to cast some relief for his senses. I stopped looking for Robert. Though he must've looked for me, as if I might appear like paper before his pen.

Sungho used a softer voice with me than before. He opened the dry cleaners in Irvington. The cleaners was steady. "During a war, the cleaners will stay open like a church," he said, "because it helps people feel clean." Four years later, when Sungho put the cleaners up for sale, bids were coming in high, and he asked me what I wanted to do. "People are drowning in hospital bills because of their aging parents," he said. "My mother gave us a gift— leaving so quickly. She was always a tidy person." Sungho spoke frankly, in a way he never would have if Huran were alive. We stopped going to church. Mass had gaps in the pews, new families came. The seats felt cold, hard. Children in the room with the glass window cried in a flock. I made no effort to think up an excuse for walking out after Eucharist.

"What's keeping us here?" I asked him.

Sungho didn't dismiss my thoughts as he used to.

"I know it's been unbearable for you," he said. "You've done enough for us." It was the closest to an apology I'd heard from him. His neck curved toward me in a light that opened like a cataract. Without Huran, I began to feel as if my time with her and Sungho might've been nothing but a nightmare.

"Do you want to move up north?" he asked.

"We can start over somewhere it rains."

"Tell me where to go, Insuk." Then he brought his hand up to his mouth. "I just don't know anymore." Looking at Sungho, it seemed as if his bones had a lightness to them like a cricket, and he raised his wings, striking the sound of what could be the first of many right decisions he would make for us both.

~

SUNGHO WAS FORTY-THREE WHEN I found a rotten tooth.

Sungho leaned in to kiss me at the door, and a stench came from his mouth. The inside looked like one house with all its lights off. A tooth cost two hundred dollars; a temporary one cost sixty. There were years we didn't have sixty dollars. On the way to the dentist I asked him, "Why didn't you tell me about your tooth?"

Oak trees reflected on the windshield.

"It's not a problem," he said.

"Your mother hated stinky breath."

"Did she?" Sungho stared out the window of the passenger seat. "I don't think she ever told me."

"Your mother hated the smell of pork. I had to clean and boil it three times. Twice wasn't enough." I relaxed my grip on the wheel—I'd known Huran better than anyone.

"You sound just like her."

"How did you ignore it? The worst pain," and I showed him three fingers, "comes from your eyes, mouth, and crotch. You can't do anything but lie there."

"I just lived with it," and he grinned. "Like I do with you."

When I parked in the lot, the sun was on its descent between the buildings. "Stop joking around," I said. "Tell me what's going on, Sungho."

"I wasn't letting my tooth fester. I was making friends with it." Sungho refrained from speaking further because of his stinking mouth.

"I probably would've never known until they found an infection inside your skull."

Sungho followed my footsteps over the asphalt, porous like black coals. His tongue poked around his mouth.

"Your tooth," I said. "We're taking it out today."

"We can't save it?"

"You want to keep your infected tooth?"

"It wasn't infected until a few days ago. It's a part of me, you know," he said. "It's natural to feel this way."

My laughter caught me by surprise.

"The worst pain comes from your heart." He put a fist over his chest. "I'm lonely—I think I need driving lessons. Can you be my driving instructor?"

I slapped his arm lightly. "Are you flirting with me? Lucky for you, your mother wouldn't let anyone get between us but herself. Especially no driving instructor."

Sungho paused at the door. "If we do leave, you think Henry will come with us?"

"Love goes in one direction," I said. "Parents love their children more than their children possibly can."

Sungho puffed his chest. "If he doesn't want to come, at least he doesn't have a gaping hole in his tooth!"

"Fine," I said. "He's a little better off than you." I took Sungho inside, both of us bowing before the door closed behind us.

It must've been during college, walking along the riverbank, when we last spoke so openly with each other, as if we no longer had to speak through the gauze we'd wrapped over our faces these past years. That night I did something I'd never done before and opened my purse and bought Sungho a shiny gold tooth.

~

IN THE SPRING, I set out a plate of yellow-ringed melon, and the movers popped the slices into their mouths. When I remarked what few things I owned in the end, they told me how people brought nothing into this life and took nothing when they left. They drove from Tacoma back to California, like whales leaving for another ocean. A port city along Washington's Puget Sound, fifty miles from Mount Rainier, Tacoma powered heavy-duty trucks, ships, and trains. The smell of sulfur came from the tideflats, the mills and refineries. Museums opened downtown, and storefronts had signs up for leasing. Newly paved roads had white paint, like gleaming bones in an X-ray.

The house was two stories with three bedrooms, two bathrooms, a garage, and a sloping lawn. To gather light, I hung mirrors on the walls; Sungho added shadows—an antique clock, a leather recliner, and a dark ottoman. I felt sorry about how I thought so little of Henry when I was with Sungho. Unlike your child, your husband stayed under your care. Most days were occupied by Sungho's shoulders, the corner of his mouth, rising and falling, and the impact of his footsteps on the stairs. Sungho looked past the vaulted ceiling, at some clot of darkness, and asked the question that was most on his mind these days: "You think Henry will come? Where do you think he goes?"

I smiled at Sungho through the arched mirror by the doorway. Mirrors tended to exaggerate smiles. "Henry's favorite thing in the world," I said, "is the world."

Sungho settled into his recliner, keeping the remote in hand. "It's like watching my father as a boy growing up to become himself," he said. "And I can't do anything about it."

The TV interrupted us. Multiple news stations reported an inter-Korean summit. Leaders of the two Koreas had met for the first time since the armistice. They had declared plans for two provinces in a united Korea with a central authority.

Sungho switched it off.

"What're you doing?" I asked.

"Let's go for a swim."

"It was important, Sungho."

Sungho approached me, and when I pushed him away, his laughter came from across the room. "Let's go for a swim."

"Fine," I said. "I could go for a swim." His palm followed the rail as he went upstairs. I heard him rummaging through a box.

Sungho dangled swim shorts over the banister. "It's a white flag," and he waved his shorts. "Do you see it?"

"That's just ugly—you're ugly."

"Every sock has a pair, no matter how ugly!"

I accused Sungho of changing into a playful person now that we'd moved into a house perched atop a hill. The first floor of the townhome lay beneath the ground at a dip in the road. As we moved aboveground, a part of Sungho was unearthed.

Sungho came downstairs and took my hand. He ran my knuckles against his stubble, sizzling like jeon in the pan. "It tickles, you idiot," and I pushed him again.

We recognized after twenty years the thrill in our chests as we chased and groped our way through the rooms of the house. We refused to hear reason and toppled the sofa and the recliner, running and giggling in the air as thick as makgeolli, as if we were rushing after our tied-up beer cans that had broken loose on the rocks and drifted down the river, but that was a long time ago, and now it was just us, in the hours passing smoothly like flour through a sifter, and the woolly bushes tapping against our windows, and there was his one golden tooth shining a single narrow path in my direction.

PUSHING THROUGH THE DOORS, we left the house together, walking down the road on careful feet. Shorts and swimsuit in hand. Our shadows deepened by roof-lines overhead. We followed the streetlamps, the smeared silvery light. We matched our pace, the only people on the slope toward the beach. We huddled together despite the warmth of the night and the width of the pathway, leaving no space between us as we headed down the steep hill. "You remind me of somebody," I said.

Sungho raised an eyebrow. "Is that so?"

"A sweet boy I met a long time ago."

"What was he like?"

"Well, he was a nice boy."

"Are you sure?"

"He was tall and handsome."

"He does sound familiar."

"What're you doing in a place like this?"

"I'm looking for a nice girl."

"Is that right—for how long?"

"Two decades, maybe."

"I was here on the beach," I said.

"We must've just missed each other."

Sungho's hands wandered under my shirt.

"I thought you were a nice boy."

"I'm a very nice boy," he said.

Sungho led me with urgency to where we heard the trees, the waves. Overhead, the crows appeared as if they were sliding down an invisible wire. A heron stood on a post above the beach. No one was on the coastline. We stripped and bore the wind and its cursive around us. We stepped into the water, waded past the dock, and we floated apart, not saying a word, then worked our way back, welding the space between us, staring at the deep blue soaking the beams, the sand, our bodies. He lifted me in the water, and my legs circled his middle, drawing him closer.

As the lights on the distant islands went out, whole cities seemed to float away. Like moths that lit up when they fluttered into a fire—death must light us up for God to notice. The deeper water filled me with guilt as I came to see how it could've been that, for years, I wouldn't help Sungho without the reminder he was less than me, and meanwhile, Sungho must have been longing for me all the same. I pulled back to take a breath. The way he pressed himself into my belly and against my hips—his face sharp with yearning. All those years, I must have believed Sungho was cruel, but when left alone, his joy was larger than my body.

I2

JENNIE

San Jose, 2000

THINGS HAD CHANGED AND JENNIE HAD KNOWN IT
was coming. The sun could barely touch the horizon and
yet considering all that happened—could it only have been
three weeks? Her muscles tore through their husks, and
she felt the ache of her dry throat and angry breasts, their
webbed veins, her swollen ankles impossible to fold, her
belly hardened with what she tried to understand. Every
night the baby breathed underwater, curled up in the whorl
of a mollusk, stealing the plums and apricots she craved,
until she passed out in a slumber, trapped in halogen night-
mares. Jennie woke up to her head splitting like a raw egg

in a condor's claws. It was during one of those days her arms and legs throbbed as if they were tearing apart. But swimming in the lagoon, crowding inside her van, brawling on the sand. The whole time Jennie was falling in love. Revisiting that day with Henry sent the same chills through her. When he shook his hair out, the strands caught in the sweep of autumn wind. Jennie was twenty when at last the baby showed its smooth honey face.

~

AFTER THE NIGHT AT the lagoon, Jennie found him, midday, leaning against his bike on the racks after coming back with a duffel bag of his things at his feet. Jennie led him to her electric-green van parked on the turnout. Henry's voice followed her to the door. "You live here alone?" She nodded, and said no one had seen it before. Henry hopped onto the foldout steps and skipped ahead of her, like a hummingbird just out of reach. The van was spacious inside. She had converted it into a study and kitchen that folded into the walls, with extendable bar tops on metal arms. Tucking the LEDs, she revealed a woodblock counter and, underneath it, a rolling cabinet fridge. The bodywork of the outfitted interior swiveled around her, jolting close and away, thrumming with essentials, anchored as an ecosystem of interlocking parts built over years. How she navigated the inside must have intrigued him.

Jennie retrieved a plastic jug of cold broth. Poured it into two stainless steel bowls off the dish rack in the overhead storage. Sound rushed from the propane system.

She put on boiling water, added thin noodles. On a makeshift board, she chopped cucumber and pear, peeled boiled eggs.

Jennie shrugged off his hands. "How long are you staying?"

Henry sat on the bench. "For a while—if you want."

She heard him say he'd leave one of these days. "For a while?" she asked. "Won't your parents look for you?"

Tossing his duffel onto the seat, he was unpacked. "My mother doesn't look for anyone but my father. It's a good thing," and he pointed his chin at the board. "Is that mulnaengmyeon?"

Jennie wiped the bowls with a dishrag. She betrayed no more signs of concern and showed her excitement. "This broth will shoot straight up your meridian."

After a dip in the boiling water, the potato-starch noodles were rinsed under the faucet. Fistfuls she twirled like hair and dropped into the bowls, splashing the broth over the steel sides. Making light work, she arranged the toppings.

"Tell me what you think," she said.

Mulnaengmyeon was a North Korean specialty. Siberian weather and mountains suited root vegetables. Those who'd fled during the war packed their taste for cold noodles, then whipped the horses and oxen to start. The delicacy was served in steel bowls with a tangy iced broth, topped with ribbons of cucumber, radish, sweet pear, a well-boiled egg, and noodles so long their lives couldn't be cut short. Jennie thought of it whenever she sprawled on the summer grass.

Henry picked up the bowl in his palms and slurped, using the chopsticks to tow the noodles and toppings into his mouth.

On his face was a keen joy, accompanied by a shudder—his head tipped back to down the rest of the broth.

Jennie set her empty bowl on the counter.

He breathed deep into his lungs. "It's sweet."

"Morioka reimen." North Korean refugees had fled to Morioka in Japan and opened mulnaengmyeon shops. "We were too poor for mulnaengmyeon in the North," she said. "So I didn't know mulnaengmyeon had sugar. They leave it out in the South. But the funny thing is the sugar stayed in Japan. The Japanese cooks at Yaohan showed me."

"My father complains that Japanese food is too sweet," he said. "But mulnaengmyeon is sweet."

"First time I had mulnaengmyeon the way it's supposed to taste was right here in the US—the place I learned about through stereotypes. *Don't go near a mall, everybody shoots each other, multiple wives, Bible-thumping fanatics*—but a consensus that—*the world would be hell without American rock music.*"

Jennie rolled the refrigerator in and slid the desktop over the counter. Pulled in the screens, fixed the hinges. Tapped a monitor to her left. She enlarged the Korean peninsula. "You Koreans call a Korean person a Han-in," then she gestured to the North. "But I grew up a Joseon-in. Joseon was the last kingdom on the peninsula before the Japanese." She centered the border between the Koreas. "From here down, you use Korean words adapted from English because of Americans. We don't do that. The North preserves our Korean. It's why a North Korean never wonders whether they're Korean."

Henry pointed to himself: "Han-in."

"Joseon-in."

For the Korean language, he said: "Hangeul."

"Joseongeul."

"There's an elegance to it."

"All this is to say—Robert wants this feeling most of all," she said. "Someone like Robert is obsessed with being seen as himself and without question."

Henry frowned at his steel bowl.

"Robert knows his options. Nukes and assassinations are out. Invasions are dangerous. Puppet leader is gone. North Korean spring is slow. He needs a South Korean spring," she said. "You saw his flag of the whole peninsula. But a flag like that doesn't change what happened—it erases what happened." Jennie tapped the ringing bowls. "This is something new. Something we haven't seen before. And it doesn't erase the past. It keeps the past with us as we go forward."

Morioka reimen summoned for Jennie what she imagined as the cocoon taste of the world she had left behind, like the wallpaper of hand-drawn flowers at her apartment outside Pyongyang, coated with a patina throughout the years. The apartment and its wallpaper conjured the carrel of lives that passed through, and the sharp taste inside the steel bowl reflected an impossible condition of life, when all that toughness and suspicion had come down on her so young that she had little memory of her childhood, except how one can cry from a thousand eyes, how in the midst of human destruction, full-toned voices broke into song, each of them apart from and a part of longing and hesitation and indignation, roiling to an intensity of hope.

Henry closed his eyes. "What about—beautiful?"

"You mean the word?"

"Areumdaweo."

Jennie, standing over him, traced the characters for *areumdaweo* on the crown of his head. The shapes resembled a lake, a fire, a house, and a person. "Henry-ya," she said, "the word for beautiful is always the same."

~

JENNIE WAS FEELING NAUSEOUS and couldn't recall the last time she had felt sick. When Henry asked her what she thought about living together in the van, she smiled to encourage him. Henry must've not been aware of her condition because he asked again, and she was careful to say nothing. Actually she was sure he didn't know because he wandered the lagoon in a daze. Though she liked the van and the feelings that came with it, she stepped out to loosen her body. Time slowed, the hours throttled back.

The sun was high. Armadillo-skinned palms dropped pods onto the windshields of parked cars. Baby palms like feather dusters stood along the asphalt where crows mowed the road for scraps.

Jennie asked whether he planned on going to college, and he rubbed his hands as if to light her question on fire. She couldn't tell what he was thinking. For some reason, she had a feeling he would wander too far—yet it was his slippery nature, like a minnow in the water, that drew her to him. When she asked too many questions, Henry would seat her on the handlebars of his bike, between his arms, and coast along Stevens Creek. Laughter pitched them forward. Either his wheels were going or his mind was going, and there was no middle point. At eighteen, it was for pleasure that Henry carved a path all over the city, his silhouette lurching through stark hills and long-haired ferns, yielding to soft mudslides.

Jennie moved the van closer to shore. She gripped the wheel with her nails. She put on the radio and hurtled through the local stations. The rearview mirror, a square sun on the dash. They passed a row of metal-plated awnings. Jennie excused herself and walked to a portable toilet. She pushed her stomach, forced the food out. Whole afternoons she ached from her toes up. Her throat felt scorched. As she walked with Henry toward the water, she realized how close they'd become. She couldn't imagine trying to hold on to him, or ridding herself of the baby. She picked up her thoughts and didn't set them down again. "If you have to go," Jennie said, "at least tell me about them."

Henry slipped into the surf. "My parents? They'd like you more than they like me," he said. "After living here so long, they like anybody but South Koreans."

This gave the impression his parents were losing their minds, but Jennie nodded. "I like them already," she said, watching him floating on the lagoon. "With you from the South and me from the North, what does that make us?"

The waves broke and frothed the air.

Henry took long strides out of the water toward her. "Mulnaengmyeon."

"With sugar," she said.

When it was dark, they huddled in a sleeping bag on the sand. They watched the moon ripen. It was prolonged in a clear sky. There was no sound at first. But his breathing became shallow. When she turned, his hand was a shadow above her waist. Jennie felt the gap between them close, and her touch became desperate, her arousal a balm for her nausea. Henry seemed so willing to disappear, like he didn't mind being no one or nothing at all. He was free above all from himself. The long night stretched its legs into dawn. Ants crossed the grains in their miniature life. The ochre light left braids in his hair. Jennie peered over as he fell asleep, his face a rumpled patch of grass.

~

AT FIRST LIGHT JENNIE called him into the van. She took the bench while he stood at the door. Jennie told him to watch the screen.

The news broke that some time ago the Korean leaders had met at an inter-Korean summit. Separated families had been reunited in Pyongyang and Seoul. Topics on the agenda included ending the war and reunification. The news focused on a second historic event—the leaders supposedly had bowls of mulnaengmyeon, separately or together. Across the country long lines of people were waiting at mulnaengmyeon restaurants. Thousands had closed after running out of ingredients. Grocery stores had sold out of noodles. People were hawking radishes outside the stations. There was a newfound hunger for peace.

Henry had chopsticks in his right hand, twirled noodles as shiny as vinyl and dragged them into his mouth.

"My dad talks about a place inside where no one can reach you. I just thought he sounded like a lonely man." He pointed at the screen. "But it's the opposite. I think it's a real place he's talking about—back home where he grew up."

"Of course," Jennie said, "Even the bleak architecture from the North still feels like home. My parents told me when I was a kid that if the country ever reunited, they'd never go South, there was nothing there for them, and they were right. Those reporters, those people don't know. They can open the border, but it'll still be there."

Henry dumped his bowl in the sink.

Jennie said to him, "You're running away, aren't you?" She couldn't stop him from going, and he couldn't keep himself here. Henry grabbed the pitcher of broth out of the fridge. He chugged it and chucked it over his shoulder. Joy shattered across his face in slow-motion like a windowpane, and she didn't know, until now, that she needed to see it. The sun hit Henry's skin like it did the water, passing through him, but left changed on the other side.

"I'm going home," he said. "Come with me, Jennie."

13

TOMOKO

San Francisco, 2001

TOMOKO, A TICKET AGENT AT SAN FRANCISCO
International Airport, dealt with her hallucinations by iden-
tifying them on her phone. At a young age, she learned that
a person she hallucinated didn't transfer onto a device. For
her job interview, Tomoko had talked to an agent for thirty
minutes before she checked her phone for the first time and
opened the camera, where the interviewer's image couldn't
be seen. When the actual interview began, she had prac-
ticed enough to not suggest she had any problems. Tomoko
worked the counter since she could keep her computer
camera on to tell whether people and things approaching

her lane were in her mind, or in reality. So when Tomoko spotted the man who matched the description on her watch list, she waved him to her lane, where the fortysomething in a gray suit with a messenger bag appeared clearly on her screen. She glanced up from his passport.

"You're quite handsome," she said, and he was, despite the harsh penalty listed under his name.

Robert seemed to consider her. Tomoko was simple-looking with a raindrop face. "Is that so?" and he set his bag down. "Thought I'd make it to the gate at least."

"Looks like your first trip back to Korea," and Tomoko read to him: "You've been *flagged as reasonably suspected to be, or have been, engaged, preparing for, or aiding in work as articulable as a potential risk or threat to national security.*"

"I can be a terror," he said, "but I'm no terrorist."

"That's pretty funny," and she smiled. "They should've put that in here. There's some good news."

"What could possibly be good about this?"

"I bet you didn't know anyone cared about you."

Robert grinned and told her it was inappropriate to flirt with a terrorist—a word she corrected to a fraud.

Tomoko stayed behind the counter with her finger over the call button for the security guards. Two guards stood nearby. "Your *current resident status has been terminated*, and you're being *deported for crimes of moral turpitude.*"

On her screen, Robert asked, "For my newspaper?"

His real question was: Would he survive? But a question whose answer depended on chance was not worth asking at all.

"Security will escort you to your gate."

"And what do you think waits for me in Korea?"

"They'll transfer you to a prison is my guess."

Tomoko found no reason to partake in his reality. Her awareness, and not her ignorance, put her in a furnace of indifference. Who did he expect her to be, this woman at the airline counter with a smile? He couldn't recognize Tomoko apart from his own imaginings. She wasn't a CIA agent, a salesman, a spy, or a person with ideals. Tomoko was a ticket agent, that was all.

Robert unbuttoned his suit jacket, stared at Tomoko, and said, "I've been invited to speak at the Busan convention hall. I must qualify for humanitarian work travel."

"You don't qualify for immunity."

"I won't go to prison for this."

Without warning, Robert reached across and grabbed her. He flung Tomoko over the counter and dropped her on her side.

She heard him break for the moving walkway.

Tomoko's head pounded. She didn't feel she was in any danger, only surprised. When she pulled herself up to the counter, she used her computer to watch the whole thing. Tomoko understood nothing was true if it could not accompany something that showed on a device.

Two agents tackled Robert before he could touch the moving walkway, its rubber belt sliding over metal rollers that groaned underfoot, onlookers, connecting between terminals or lugging bags across concourses, stopping to watch, crowding him, visibly stimulated by his head smashing into the floor, the man muffled but wriggling and warbling, his complexion pale, his body wrangled up, his arms cuffed behind him, and the way he flung his dreams into the air, called the name of a woman, his mother or his lover, until the stun guns came out, and their bright silver mandibles clicked into place, making a gourd-shaped stain on his pants.

Mouth slack, he was trying to button his suit closed, but his arms wouldn't reach, so he shouted that he wished to button his suit, then begged for somebody to do it, and even then he was handsome, the dark furrows of his brows, the bridge of his nose, and from farther away came the booted footsteps of police, bins knocked over, the airport vehicle brakes screeching, their radios bleating, yellow tape on the tarmac. Tomoko watched her blank reflection on the screen, grinding her teeth as she did in her sleep, her fingers pressing into her brain, synapses branching, thrumming, spinning as she counted the people who stopped to watch the handsome man, not a hundred, or even a thousand, but more like one zero zero zero zero zero.

ROBERT

ROBERT ARRIVED AT THE western end of the demilita-
rized zone, the border between North and South Korea,
one hundred sixty miles long and two and a half miles
wide while morning mist still guarded the watchtowers.
Robert had lived to smell the tidal marshes, rich and damp
off the rains from the monsoon season. A red-crowned
crane, early for winter, stood idly as if on a wall screen or a
celadon vase in a museum. They had put him on a civilian
plane, a cargo train, then an armored vehicle, and after a
day and a half, Robert was looking at farmlands. He had
only heard rumors of political prisoners who were interned
in farming villages surrounded by barbed-wire fences.

Hours after his arrival, the South Korean guards
escorted Robert off the farmlands and across torqued wires
to the border station and its baby blue meeting rooms.
When he stumbled on a craggy incline, the guards fixed
his shoelaces. And when he looked out from the trail, the
guards paused for him. A wildlife refuge naturally sprang
from a place without humans. The flora and fauna rooted
themselves in the primordial land. But within miles, armies
on both sides could bombard each other at ten thousand
rounds a minute. The guards let him inside a meeting room.
They popped the cuffs off him, ignoring security measures,
and went out, locking the door behind them.

When it opened again, the first guard, who towered above him, appeared, folding away an application to gain entry. The second guard, with sunburned cheeks, rolled in a utility cart with equipment covered by a black tarp. The equipment would've arrived by train crossing the Imjin and been transferred onto a bus to the civilian-restricted area. The first guard asked the second guard why they shouldn't have a little fun, and the second guard said why not. They parked the mysterious equipment against the wall and left the room.

Robert's attention went to the warm, lined corner where he could sleep. He recalled that his mother and father shared their names with their countrymen just as those across the border, outside his windows, shared their names with him. Robert remembered events by their years, and bodies by their numbers. When he counted these things together, the sum amounted to nothing but a haze. It could be that all memory of Korea came from the border, and the farther you were from the border, the more your memory faded like a coyote who looked back just once before running off into the forest.

~

AT A GRAVELLY, scraping sound, the door shoved open by a wild boar that walked into the room sniffing the floor. Muscles tight, Robert shot up. He was certain the boar weighed more than him. Layers of black-brown hair, upright ears, reddish around its trotters and snout. Stench of garbage like the wild boars on Jeju Island, which had often roamed in packs and damaged crops when he was a boy. The boar tugged off the tarp, revealing not just any equipment but arms for the Republic of Korea Army.

Robert knew what he was looking at, more or less, but these were new models. There was an assault rifle, a machine gun, and a pistol, and the fourth was also a machine gun using an advanced system. The assault rifle and the first machine gun were familiar from his time in the army, but the pistol and the second machine gun had lighter, solid frames with matte finishes. The boar poked around. Its snout moved independently of its face. Robert scrambled to the far corner, where he stood as the third point of a triangle formed by the boar, the arms, and himself.

Robert turned the situation over in his mind. The guards could be asking Robert to shoot the boar. They might want to see if he could use the arms. They might want to see what he would do before deciding what to do with him. They had left no instructions. Perhaps they feared how Robert would react if he were to be liberated. What if he sought vengeance? How could they measure his desperation? When Robert arrived in his own country, he had stepped onto enemy territory. Many people had taunted him for coming back home. The dust, swirling under the waning sun, settled onto his eyelashes.

~

WHEN THE TWO GUARDS appeared again, they ignored him and the tarp, and crossed the room to the boar. Then the guards were on their knees, scratching the boar's belly, cooing in gentle tones. They brushed its long-haired chin and tasseled legs. The first guard took a fistful of beans out of his pack and fed the boar. As the boar grunted and spat, the second guard tried an impersonation but was scolded by the first guard for insulting the boar as it was eating—a cause for indigestion. The second guard nestled his nose into the boar's side as it munched ripe beans off his palm. The guards fussed over its crusted eyes, its brittle canines, asking after its well-being, to which it replied by sniffing their packs.

The second guard handed Robert a change of clothes and lured the boar outside, where they waited for him.

The guards had left him again with the military equipment.

Robert dressed quickly and came out, squinting at the midday sun. He followed the guards' footsteps and the boar's moonsteps to the ridge, where he could see in the distance a husband and wife and three children touring the grounds. The border had a strict dress code, but the family wore tattered jeans and sweaters. The North often captured footage of tourists in torn apparel as propaganda to show the South's failings. The guards, however, waved to the tourists jovially. The guards explained that times were changing and that the family's attire had government approval.

Robert, the guards, and the boar arrived at a field.

The first guard, staring at the field's edge, said, "Can we call you Rob?" The name fell easily out of his mouth.

The second guard stood a few strides away, showing regard for Robert's space. "Even all the way here at the DMZ, we've heard of you."

Robert was surprised when told of the distance his words had traveled, holding him to some esteem.

The field was overgrown—soft if he were to kneel in it. "The guns are for me," Robert said. "I was suspicious, but I figured it was true when you left me in the room to change this morning."

Robert went on, "At the start, I thought I was supposed to shoot the boar," and this made the guards chuckle. "The boar is your pet that just happened to wander in. You never planned for the boar. You treat it too well to let me shoot it."

The first guard brushed the boar's ears. "Isn't that so?"

"No mistakes so far," the second guard said.

"You put guns in the room to see if I'd run. When I didn't run, you agreed on something," Robert said. "I could be a lure. I could lure people out when I announce my arrival."

The second guard nodded. "I do believe in good timing." His eyes shot up. "We want to help you. Your mission is nice and simple: Some dangerous people are bound to show at your lecture in Busan. Shoot one down, and you're free to go."

"No prison, no internment," the first guard said.

"It can be anybody. The target is your choice," the second guard said. "But you only catch a tiger by going into its cage."

"What about me?" Robert asked. "Aren't I dangerous?"

"Rob, you're harmless." The first guard spoke words Robert had never heard before. "You're not a political figure, and you're not that radical. You're a revolutionary from the old days. But in this day and age, you're a person with a conscience, that's all." The guard had lined up a cue stick and split a pyramid on a pool table, and each of Robert's life choices clattered in every direction.

"You still make good points in your paper," the second guard reassured Robert. "Don't kick yourself over it. You're going to be out of here. You do this, and it'll squash any protestors and any doubt about you going free," and he slapped his back. "And don't worry about what happens. You just try your best, Rob."

"You can choose a gift for the road," the first guard said. "We make guns now. They're indigenous. Daewoo Precision Industries K2 assault rifle—standard service rifle. Shoulder-fired, gas-operated. Fires both the .45 and .223."

"We started design and development years ago," the second guard said. "The K2 you see with the pistol grip and side-foldable buttstock? It goes semiauto, three-round, fully automatic." He made a gesture for sewing his mouth closed. "We sell them to Cambodia, Ecuador, Fiji, Indonesia, Iraq, Lebanon, Mexico, Nigeria, Peru, Philippines. North Korea's even made dupes of them. What a compliment!"

"The K2 works fine, probably shocking for you to hear, but it does have an overheating problem," the first guard said. "K3 is the light machine gun. They modernized it, underside rails, side-folding stock, carbon fiber shield.

South Africa and Thailand like them. Asian arms manufacturers are finally getting ahead of Western ones."

"Daewoo," Robert said. "They make cars, don't they?"

The second guard smirked. "Motor vehicles division's big, but they oversee tanks and arms production. Military invents everything civilians use. The military budget funded the internet for the front lines. First mobile phones were used in the army. Things get made mostly by the companies you hear about, and they find their way back to the commercial market because civilians want to buy our cool shit."

The second guard seemed composed until he came to the last two weapons in the series. "That pretty K5 you saw in there is a semiautomatic pistol. Compact, lightweight, fast-action trigger for accurate shots. And I mean accurate. The frame is forged from aluminum alloy, and it has a matte finish. The slide and barrel, forged from steel, with a right twist. On the market, Americans love it. They like the sexy look." The second guard chuckled. "The K7 is my favorite. It's our submachine gun with an integral suppressor. We got the idea from our special forces lot. Takes standard or subsonic ammo. Simple, clean blowback system. We finished it in December. Let's just say people are going to shit themselves at the IDEX."

The first guard rolled his eyes. "If you're done touching yourself, we can get on with the show."

The second guard said to Robert, "One body in the ground will do, but you should protect yourself. It's your lecture, buddy."

Across the field, they could see the North Korean guards pacing the border. The first guard said, "Looking at them is like looking into the past. Sometimes your past smiles at you. Other times your past points a gun at you." The first guard went on in a firm voice, "Don't get stuck in the old world. You're waking up to the new one. We don't do things like we used to. We're not even the same people. You go out there and say what you're going to say, and you'll see. You'll get treated worse than a dog," and he shook his head. "The only people who understand you are right here, where you don't want to look. We see, as clear as day, who you are. Because we are you, except we stayed back home. We don't need any more businessmen or leaders," he said. "What we need is a good man."

I4

ROBERT

Busan, 2001

THE NATION HELD ITS BREATH THE FOLLOWING summer as the president of South Korea won the Nobel Peace Prize for his Sunshine Policy toward North Korea. Exiled and kidnapped, he'd protested the government and its dictatorial rule, issuing an antigovernment manifesto, and was locked up before being released two years later, designated a "prisoner of conscience" by Amnesty International. With a vocational high school education, he coolly won against an elite opponent with an advanced degree, and was elected into the Blue House, where he dawned the Sunshine Policy for the reunification of the Korean states. It recognized two different systems, militaries, and foreign policies, with relations to be managed by inter-Korean organizations until unification could bring about a federal system of one people, two regional governments. North Korea didn't oppose the presence of US troops on the peninsula for protection, keeping China at bay. After the peace summit, during the Olympic ceremony, the Korean Unification Flag was trotted into the stadium. On a white flag, a blue silhouette of the Korean peninsula. The pale cloth flashed. Robert had waited decades for the flag to wave across LED screens at train stations and bars, markets and apartments. Everywhere people watched. They gazed at the flag the way you might gaze into the younger faces of your parents and recognize yourself.

~

AFTER FOUR DAYS, the guards released Robert in an armored vehicle, and instead of sending him to a prison, they kept their word and put him on a bus headed south, and then a train to the city. Outside the station, Robert rented a car to drive farther south along the coast to Busan, following the dock houses and seafood markets. Over two hundred fifty miles later, Robert pulled up in front of the convention hall in Busan where he'd originally planned a lecture on his writings. His words from *Liberation Shinmun* had traveled to these shores, and the invitation by locals was something to be proud of. More than the prestige, the rarity of this conference was supposed to draw out a network of people who would spend an evening discussing his views. In front of the main auditorium, Robert could see journalists and news cameras, tipped off by protests against reunification that had taken place ahead of his arrival. Perhaps Robert wouldn't motivate anyone, but he had to use what would be his last chance to speak to his countrymen. Sitting in the darkness of the car, Robert dreamed of an impossible evening in which common sense prevailed. However, instead of the many pages of his writings, Robert found in his bag a single loaded gun.

JENNIE

JENNIE DROVE THE VAN north from San Jose past the townhomes of Milpitas and Ohlone College and through the valleys where stiff yellow grass could threaten smoke even in the cold. These days, Jennie couldn't sleep, her hands clammy and blankets corkscrewed, or she jolted awake as if birds had tangled themselves inside her. There was a steeliness in her bones—all molars. Burning fuel, she snaked the highways. They stopped for burritos in the Mission District near the cemetery at an adobe-style restaurant. Behind the bar-top altar, old timber walls, hanging rawhide, a Spanish-style organ, a copper bell, a figure of Christ above, and, even higher than God's son, a television that Henry flipped through with a remote. The Korean news came on. Faces distorted by the force of motion, their one-way gazes, protest signs heaved out of the frame. Jennie tore each day off like a sheet from a daily calendar, watching her days grow thinner, just as she watched the older generation disappear, taking with them their connection to the border. Jennie ordered two burritos and beers.

ROBERT

STANDING IN THE WINGS of the main auditorium, Robert stared out at the reporters and journalists, students and locals, waiting in the crowd. His heart raced to see it was standing room only, even as the Mnet Music Video Festival ramped up back in Seoul with honey-voiced Jo Sungmo leading the nominees. Robert stepped onto the stage in his gray suit, which had few wrinkles because the guards had given him a change of clothes. Robert stood behind the center podium. Leaning forward, he scanned the auditorium. The guards were nowhere to be seen because they hadn't followed him. The weather stopped at the door. Security checked into the pit. Crowds pushed onto the floor. Greetings shot across the aisles. Flash orbs had eyes like tree knots. Shadows flew up and shattered across the ceiling.

Robert looked out at hundreds of his countrymen. Through their cameras, thousands. Behind him a projection illumed a flag of the Korean peninsula. Clicks fired in the cavernous space. Light barreled toward him. Their lenses captured him, as if he were a common fly suspended inside of a glass jar. Robert noticed how tired he must be to sway from a slight breeze. So he began: "We watched colonial empires crumble here and around the world. And with them, the reprehensible beliefs that raised them. We grew up against the backdrop of war. A war as militant as it was ideological—and we've observed little difference between the ways we've approached war. Still, there has been progress in our small country and in our standing in the greater world. Yet it was when I left Korea that I was free to be Korean."

JENNIE

JENNIE, WATCHING THE NEWS at the bar in the Mission, caught a few seconds of a clip, and she could have sworn it was Robert. It was Robert's voice, but he looked narrower, the main light source above him throwing his shadows left and right. Henry jerked out of his seat. He was still in his swim shorts, despite the chilly air, his head sinking as he leaned over the bar. Hearing Robert's words rather than seeing them on a page, she found some sense in them. Jennie could feel the heat radiating from the screen, like a corpse burning on temple grounds. Jennie popped the burrito from its aluminum seal. A shot of the audience showed faces dusted by stage glow. Black eyes, swallowing light. Bent arms, or camera props. Jennie couldn't stop from gorging on the flesh of the tortilla. As if under the husk was her salvation, retrieved not with guns and knives but with teeth. Smiling, laughing, she slapped the bar top and broke into a howl.

ROBERT

THE AUDIENCE CLAPPED. Those in seats or standing in aisles chuckled, and they wouldn't have if they knew what Robert was going to say. He pawed the wrist that had been bothering him since the airport.

"The South Korea and Japan match at the 1997 World Cup qualifier—in Tokyo of all places," and hoots came from the auditorium. "That's right. Early in the second, Japan chipped the ball over Korea's keeper. We thought it was over. Japan only had to protect their lead. But Korea scored a corner with a header. Now we're a moral 1–1. Time's running out. Suddenly, Korea fires a left footer into the back of the net." Robert's arms shot up, cheers erupted. "It's called the Greatest Battle in Tokyo. It's just a soccer game—a fucking game. My God, we lost so badly after that game, but who cares. For a moment, everybody was Korean. You were Korean because of your love for humans everywhere."

Robert glanced at the projection. "For one day, this was our flag. Nobody saw a line," he said. "Maybe I'm a fool. Why visit the past, why go digging up its grave? Why puncture a sense of safety we've carefully built for ourselves? Why not go on toward the things we know we can keep? We know what a home feels like and we can have one. We know what a family feels like and we can make one." Robert thought of that night at the pool hall. It could be that Sungho believed freedom was only an idea, and an idea didn't keep you alive. Yet they each had the freedom to choose their own way of seeing the world.

His voice reached the doors. "We remember the US picked a line at the thirty-eighth parallel, dividing Korea in half. North to the Soviets, South to the US. Millions of innocents dead in the war. Our problems since the border went up are growing. You know it, without me telling you tonight. The era we live in now deepens inequalities within and between nations. The consequences are landing on ordinary people and causing further divisions in wealth and policies as we grapple with discrimination, tribal nationalism, and greed."

The projection behind him changed to photographs of protesters and political prisoners stuffed by groups of ten into twenty-five-square-foot cells. It was how he pictured Ominato in northern Japan before the *Ukishima Maru* detoured into the harbor. "Looking back we now know the opportunities we've lost. Fear-driven complacency. Brittle corruption. We are making the very mistakes we've long condemned."

Robert motioned at a series of photographs from settlements under barbed wire manned by the country's soldiers. He wasn't among them. "These are the ominous parts of modernization and globalization," Robert said with a humorless grin. "Nothing works better than hatred and fear, which are, as you well know, trending and on the rise, stirring national and global competition for power.

Don't let me tell you, you can see it for yourself." Looking out at the faces, floating in the dark, the figure of Medusa occurred to him—a head of snakes. Medusa avoided mirrors to keep from turning herself into stone. Robert understood how Medusa was a fearless foe. How she was fearful above all of her own image.

Robert raised his face to the cool light of the projector. "In some ways we freed ourselves only to imprison others. As humankind, we agreed freedom is a resource with a controlled, limited supply."

~

THE SUNSHINE POLICY WAS lost in the end. There were allegations that hundreds of millions of dollars had been paid to North Korea to secure the North-South peace summit. Hyundai had transferred five hundred million dollars to the North. Critics claimed that the president had bought his Nobel Peace Prize. Hyundai testified that they'd paid for business rights in the North. They were charged anyway with violating laws on foreign trade and inter-Korean affairs. The Hyundai chairman would apologize, jowls trembling at a televised news conference. US relations with the South became strained, as if the US were scolding its lesser sibling. Future summits were deemed tainted by the financial transaction. The president's campaign, the inter-Korean summit, and the mulnaengmyeon tradition, all of it seemed like some orchestration, a performance. Few asked whether peace demanded a price. Fewer still pointed out that the policy's problem lay not with the scandal but with its purpose. The policy aided the North without improving human rights in the North. There was a misunderstanding that North Korean people starved because they needed aid. They starved because they were in need of freedom.

When nationwide suspicions about spies and sympathizers for the North had reached a crescendo, the guards had rubbed Robert's shoulders. The guards and Robert had shot the guns in the fields together. Robert could shoot into the auditorium, like he had in those fields, motivated by "conscience," and be pardoned by the government. They would give him an apartment hoisted on government land on the Seoul outskirts where he could live in heavy clothes, shod in thick boots, stomping in the snow in the winter, or running along the river in the spring, summer, and fall. Robert would write letters to Insuk about how he could see the gleaming lights of two countries. On the auditorium stage, Robert slowed his speech—his head lolled. Whether peace or war, the same or a different outcome, it didn't matter. But a still, small voice inside him seemed poised at this hour. That Jo Sungmo had won the music awards was the last thing Robert heard from the whispering crowd before he looked at the far booth into the camera's shining red light.

~

BY THE TIME THE projector showed the fourth photograph, the Gwangju protests, there was silence. Some murmurs. Discontent. Reporters and journalists took in the view. Five in the aisles and four in the rows walked out. Notepads were folded away, repurposed as fans. Media cycles wouldn't run this story. Now it was a spectacle. The people who stayed glanced sideways.

Robert wasn't asking them to abandon their lives. He was asking them for three minutes on stage.

Coughs. Someone laughed for the hell of it.

Two minutes in, he gripped his hurt wrist.

"For the moment we've lost sight of a cause to unite us." Robert needed to make them question the war and the border, and their own biases.

Robert couldn't speak in a rush, or it would all be for nothing. "I'm going to ask you a question."

Nervous laughs, a sole clap. It wasn't that Robert was articulate, but there was a satisfying element in hearing his argument fill the strange vase he presented.

The projection lit up the flag.

"I'm asking you if a divided country is still a country."

Robert turned from the crowd, crossed the stage, then made his way back, as if going through the fields of tall grass waving in his path, feet tangled in wildflowers like umbrellas unfolding, red camellias rustling, animals grazing nearby, a rippling stream ahead, a tucked-away bank, but nothing in the distance. Not his mother waiting for him, no floating debris. Nothing of Insuk's beauty through the glass door. Now of all times, he walked into the memory of an argument, when he was telling Insuk that if your leg was broken, you wouldn't cut it off, would you, you'd care for it. That's why a person, or a nation, couldn't cut itself off. Behind him was the landscape of men and women, black-eyed, muscular and tight-skinned, dead in one long breath, each having left someone unloved.

HENRY

I HEARD WATER IN my ears before I saw the bridge. I took the wheel once we crossed the strait. Off the 680, the 80 east of Auburn bisected the Tahoe National Forest. The windows I opened for the sweet pine and balmy cedar, aromatic lakes, granite, and sky. Inside the van—the deep smell of jjajangmyeon, sharp mulnaengmyeon, lagoon sand eddying in whirls, flying over the road. I thought of Robert in the private rooms of Biwon. He had talked about different kinds of losses. That those losses must be imagined to make an apology. Because an apology must also mourn a future where those losses never occurred. Robert's responsibility toward the world was not imaginary but as real and as defined as the brass fixtures of the pool hall, molded by the weight of history.

I crossed into Reno to keep east on the northbound road. By the time I looked out at Oregon, it was dark. Rain fed the mountain gulches. Mugwort in silver green. My shorts so damp I had to peel them off. I switched places with Jennie, who put a wet towel on her head. She drove seven hours through the night over the Columbia River and into Washington and then Tacoma. We covered the five kingdoms: the mineral, the vegetable, the animal, the human, and we must've passed a God between San

Jose and Tacoma. By morning, the streets were dense with cars and music. Century-old brick warehouses. A rack of clothes for sale. Smashed box of cigarettes by the storm drain. Crowds appeared, moved like weather. A biker zoomed by, strips on his spokes blinking red.

ROBERT

"I CONSIDER IT DESPICABLE." Robert stopped, winding his two fingers like blades on a waterwheel. "To use our suffering to justify our destructive actions. I won't be coerced into silence. It is precisely because I know what it is like to suffer that I will not be intimidated." He paused, and said, "If you don't feel moved by the horrors that have destroyed our past, then we are doomed in all our efforts toward the future."

One reporter said, "The idea's already been canceled and discarded by Koreans."

Another reporter agreed. "Reunification is over," he said. "It's not a viable option."

The crowd sounded far away. Outside, traffic had thinned from a standstill. Busan moved freely at ten at night. The technicians were on standby. A shrill pitch came from the speakers. Junior reporters and journalists recorded on their phones. They inched out of their seats and toward the stage.

"It'd cause innumerable deaths," a third reporter said.

Robert's shoes remained fixed to the floor. "The border is sustained by us. We choose it every day. It is a fact that we can't keep this up. Even if we've gone numb, I assure you we are dying by the day."

Robert, as a boy, heard stories about women guerilla fighters of Jeju Island, chisel-bodied in a wooden doorway, nine or ten of them, after a run on their horses from the mainland police and transporting villagers to hideouts, but never seen or heard of since. Stories about prisoners, who urinated at length and were beaten for passing signs. Even walking at an uneven pace was a form of communication. How could they erase all meaning from themselves? Yet a meaningless world didn't deprave them as much as a world whose true meaning was lost.

His voice arched over the pit. "One truth is that our capacity to hurt each other is equaled by our capacity to heal each other."

The crowd responded with disbelief. They spoke of gall and rage and defeat. They waited for his final words. Robert had built his lecture toward a reveal. And he felt their hopelessness, as if they waited for a bud to signal the spring.

When a shout broke his spell, Robert saw the red light of the camera. "We have no choice but to heal our border."

Robert pointed his toes to direct himself center stage.

For a brief moment, they must've sensed something was wrong. Security moved out of the pit. Microphones were pulled.

Two men with badges approached the stage. No words were spoken. They simply waited for Robert in the wings.

Robert wasn't afraid.

Convention hall exits were barred. The podium stumbled away from him. They just saw the top of his head bowing—a black avalanche of hair.

Robert recalled his dream of a thousand faces, and his dreams unified with reality, allowing him to see their lives as beads of air that rose through the water, like a pearl necklace, like a rosary. Somewhere their faces pendulated. Somewhere they collapsed or fell silent. Somewhere their voices floated into the rafters. Somewhere blood pumped into the mud. Somewhere a spark lit a cauldron. His mother's house on Jeju Island, the teacups at Biwon, the supermarket loading docks, the dim pool hall, the names of Busan beaches, the port outside where his mother arrived one night in 1945—the water was colder then. Now the faces dreamed of him, and it was him they recalled, and they saw Robert reach inside his suit for the whole auditorium to see.

Calmly, slowly, Robert took out the pistol. Shouts came from the back of the hall. The badges sprinted forward. Screams erupted as he aimed for his temple. Robert's last thought was how the trigger pulled with just the slightest touch of his hand.

INSUK

THAT MORNING, the bell rang, and I opened the door and found Henry with a young pregnant woman. The woman bowed and Henry followed. It was so clear outside I saw the mountains behind them. After driving hard through the night on the Pacific Highway, they had blown their engine. Henry hadn't said they were coming or how long they would stay, and I didn't ask. But the van had to go to the shop, where it must wait for a new engine. Henry changed out of his shorts and slept on the recliner. Jennie fed herself at the table. She met the bottom of every bowl with her tongue. I boiled two ramen packets, and she even drank the broth. I panfried green onion pajeon— she polished off six jeons. So I refilled the banchan from my storage, dug out my ceramic pot for abalone porridge, set it out with bibimbap and kimchi jjigae, and jaengban buckwheat noodles with perilla leaves. Jennie licked the plates before I could serve a ladle of spicy yukgaejang with eggs. When Sungho came home, he couldn't believe the dish pile. It was easy for me to take comfort in feeding her, as if my heart had taken on the shape of a spoon. It was not my son but the young woman I called to the table again, and she bounded toward me in a brilliant display of light, light, light.

IV

THE ENDLING

2010–2014

15

SUNGHO

Tacoma, 2010

AT THE DRY CLEANERS SUNGHO LEASED IN DOWNTOWN
Tacoma, he got news that his twenty-seven-year-old son
had received a callback for a desk job in Seattle. They were
looking for somebody to type on a computer without fuss.
They would note his son's diligence if he showed up in a
suit. Jennie, who worked with Sungho, reassured him she
would close that night. The cleaners took up a thousand-
square-foot space in a squat brick building shared with an
antique shop near the college campus. Jennie wasn't the sort
of person who did nothing. She was finishing her degree
program online and helping Sungho at the front desk.

Jennie was so careful she could pass through a spider's web on a line hung between Sungho and Insuk, Henry and Haru, without ever breaking it.

Sungho didn't worry about her like he did for Henry's future. After leaving the key ring with Jennie, Sungho rushed home to dress Henry in the navy pants and white shirt he had ironed himself. Sungho offered his own navy tie, but Henry changed his mind about wearing one, and Sungho decided his son was right. Sungho insisted on driving him, but Henry declined, and they walked to the bus stop. Sungho couldn't predict what Henry would need. Sungho, staring at his son's frame, made a feeble joke about his suit making him taller. "One thing I've learned is clothes meet you at every stage of your life," and Sungho could hear the wind machine against the relaxing crinkle of plastic garment bags. Baby gowns. School uniforms. Wedding tuxes. Dress shirts. Black garments. "Clothes make you feel sure of where you're going."

Sungho regretted that his wife was busy now at the beach with Haru, who had turned nine this year. Henry was almost the age of Sungho's father when he disappeared. Sungho observed his father's mark on Henry. Henry messed up his hair or untucked his shirt, as if these were traits of his own. Henry gathered magnolia leaves off the road and fanned them out like cards in his hands, as if he chose, moment by moment, the path ahead of him. Sungho sensed that something was wrong, but Henry wouldn't tell him what it was. Henry said he only did things he had to do. Sungho felt threatened by the sadness in his voice, so he told Henry that despite what he believed, if he would reconcile himself to the soft focus of a daily routine, he would not stumble but progress toward a real and concrete joy as a human being.

After Henry bused to the city, Sungho went upstairs to his son's bedroom. Jennie and Haru shared a bigger room across the hall since Haru hated to sleep alone. With his family, Henry couldn't fathom what years were speeding toward him now. It occurred to Sungho to drive Henry home, but he might embarrass his son by showing up outside the building. Normally, it would be Insuk who was concerned about Henry, but she seemed focused on Jennie, spending hours to cook her a dish for the first time. Sungho started to make the bed before he realized that Henry had done it already. The blanket folded like a hospital sheet. It was an ordinary sight, but for Henry it was unusual. It was what Sungho expected out of a son but not what he expected out of Henry. Sungho thought of his father, who left as suddenly as a note struck on a keyboard, ringing in his ears ever since.

~

SUNGHO NOTICED HENRY'S BIKE leaning against the entryway. Now in his fifties, Sungho couldn't remember when he last rode a bike. He guessed it was during college in Daejeon. Sungho took the bike down to the main road.

Letting the pedals go, the metal frame rattled. Sungho couldn't stop shaking, out of excitement. He pumped his legs at the bottom of the road. The crank going, his wheels turning. Sungho was young again—his youth a flag waving on its stand. Sungho could imagine a version of his life along the path of the bike. Sungho understood, after all these years, that his father must have longed for himself. Sungho gripped the handlebars, let the wheels loose on the corners, molding the line behind him. His eyes followed the reflectors. Then he kicked off the road into the high brush. With a hand, Sungho parted the grass to a clear view of the water at the field's edge. The dusk wore brightly colored pants—red, orange, blue, and purple.

~

IT WAS DARK OUTSIDE—no sign of Henry. Insuk stirred a pot of jjigae for when Henry came home. She seemed sensitive to the sounds of Jennie and Haru reading upstairs—her ears like coiled fiddleheads unfurling into fronds. Insuk worried it would be a waste if Henry had eaten already, and Sungho reassured her the girls would be hungry. Sungho coached Insuk on not asking too many questions after the interview. "We don't want to disappoint him if it's not good news," and he repeated it in case she hadn't heard it the first time. "If he's happy, then we can double it. If he's sad, then we must cut it in half."

Sungho switched on the porch light. Insuk told him to wait since Henry had his own way of doing things. The girls finished the jjigae before it turned cold.

Two hours passed. Sungho walked down the driveway. Streetlamps stood in nests of light. Sungho roamed farther, thinking he'd seen Henry. At the corner, no one was there.

Sungho called the downtown office. There was no answer in the middle of the night. Sungho left a message explaining that he was looking for Henry, who was supposed to have arrived that afternoon. Sungho tried again at six in the morning. At six thirty, a young man came on and put him on hold. When he came back, there was the sound of keyboard strokes and the mouse clicking as repetitious as a clock ticking beneath its lidded face. Sungho asked whether he should come in person. The young man remembered, just then, what had happened with the candidate. Henry had never showed at the interview.

~

SUNGHO DROVE A MILE down the road to the bus stop. Black, shiny trash bags lined the street. Sungho had been fooled into thinking his father's mistakes remained in the past. Sungho wanted to know whether it was his fault Henry couldn't place both feet on the ground comfortably enough to stay. Who but a son could abandon his father?

How could the girls not accuse Sungho of his disappearance? Sungho left the stop, parked on the hill, and walked to the beach.

As he stepped onto the sand, a thing buried in Sungho surfaced. Henry could've thrown himself into the sea.

Still in his clothes, Sungho leaped into the water.

Wading into the current, he caught a full wave in the face. Sungho swam on, swallowing water. He was certain he felt a wing or a branch. Sungho dove headfirst into the gray layers. His eyes stung in the water. Somebody must've seen Henry.

When Sungho came up, Insuk was tearing down the beach like a column of light. She yanked him out of the riptide and onto shore with the vigor of her years.

He couldn't hear anything until she shouted, "Henry's not in there, Sungho. He's not in there."

Sungho's heart was beating against his chest, like the tied-up boats hitting the dock. "How do you know?"

"I know a little about my son," she said. "He's not like us."

This put him at ease, and Insuk wrung out his clothes.

Insuk brought him to the car and drove them home. She washed him and hung their clothes. Insuk pressed his wrinkled fingertips. It was possible Henry would never return to them. Sungho wondered at some feeling—his father and his son walking off in broad daylight without words. It left Sungho with the question of who he had been as a son, then as a father. The shadows they cast were longer than the years.

Sungho had wanted his son to care for him as he aged— for his son to iron his clothes and dress him. For his son to complain about what a hassle Sungho had become. It was natural to return to a son after being a father. For his father, Jeha, to return to a building after being a person. "You think Henry knows," he asked, "his father's heart?" Insuk placed her hands on his throat and face—her thumb on the bud of his lower lip.

~

TWO DAYS AFTER HE searched the beach, Sungho was standing in the driveway when over the hill came Jennie and Haru hopping toward him, and between them was Henry. His son's words were difficult to make out, but his warm tones were familiar. Sungho watched them quietly from a distance. When the girls' laughter reached his ears, Sungho noticed how Jennie seemed never to have feared Henry would disappear. Haru carried a bouquet of milk-weeds and lilies. Sungho was awestruck, as if it were Jeha returning to him and his mother over the road and to the basement rental. His shirt wrapped around his head, his slacks wrinkled and cuffed at the ankles, and grinning wide, he flapped his arms, and kicked his knees higher and higher as if he could fly off in a moment, but Henry wouldn't because he wasn't Jeha, because his son would stay, because his son was a father.

16

INSUK

Tacoma, 2014

EIGHTY OR NINETY BIRDS IN A BARE MULBERRY tree in the morning, and by noon, they moved as one dark net to capture another tree in the distance. After the incident with his interview, Henry had changed to sleeping on a floor pad in Jennie and Haru's room, leaving the room across the hall empty. This room had the largest window with a decent view of the hillside, covered with wildflowers, and nobody wanted it to themselves. The fuss Huran once made over rooms almost seemed sensible. In the kitchen, Sungho asked me, "When do you think they'll need to eat again?" Sungho spoke quietly because they were asleep upstairs. "Should I run to the market?"

"It's better I stay here," I said. "Go quick."

"I'm surprised Haru hasn't asked for beer yet."

I pushed Sungho out the door. "She eats like you," and feeling pleased, said, "Haru's diapers used to be heavy, weren't they?"

"You never cook like this for me. If I'm hungry, you tell me to pick up something for myself."

"Oh, get out before they hear you whining."

Jennie had stayed in the casual way she'd come. Shortly after they'd arrived, I had asked Sungho to park her van with its new engine in the garage. Every morning for the first decade they lived with us, I took Haru to the beach to let Jennie rest. By the time Jennie came downstairs, I had her coffee on the kitchen counter. Jennie would leave to meet Sungho at the cleaners. Henry woke up around then and applied for jobs until, at Sungho's suggestion, he'd started work at the wildlife sanctuary. Henry brought back feathers, fur, and scales into the house. Haru volunteered on weekdays after school. Haru loved a tapir she described as a baby elephant mixed with a boar.

The room Jennie, Haru, and Henry shared was bigger, and they could see the shore and the pale-trunked silvering trees that sloped low as if in midfall over the road. They could smell their clothes drying in the wind. The sky lashed with deep purple and gray. When Sungho returned with groceries, he wanted to look, but I swatted him away. Maybe Jennie had arrived expecting nothing from me.

But when she appeared at my door, I came to the realization that I had been preparing a place all this time not for my son but for Jennie and Haru. The room was filled with their clean scent. A mesh of light caught them from the window. They slept like dead fish one atop the other.

~

IT WAS MID-APRIL WHEN we saw the news on TV. The ferry *Sewol* had sunk en route from Incheon to Jeju Island. The vessel was overloaded. The cargo improperly secured. Of the four hundred forty-three on board, three hundred twenty-five were high school students. As the vessel capsized and water flooded the cabins, announcements from the speakers told them to stay put. The students obeyed. But the crew escaped. The captain was seen abandoning the ship in his underwear. Footage recovered from the ship was broadcast. The faces were blurred. Their voices were changed. They were laughing for a brief second of nervous excitement. "Do you think we'll become famous," somebody said, "like the Titanic?"

Sungho urged Haru to her room, where she could ask him questions. Henry, shaking his head, left to be outside. Jennie knotted her fingers painfully. She might never have seen a thing so horrific. I rocked her—embraced her tightly with my shoulders. Haru could be heard asking why the students never jumped. Americans would've jumped. Each of us looked for answers. What happened in the pitch-black? Where could they go in the water? "If you are on a sinking ship, don't trust anybody," Sungho said. "Don't listen to anybody."

The way a ship sinks in compartments, from one partition to another, was the way a country sank. A rescue diver testified: "Now I urge the government not to seek the people's help in any disaster but to look to itself." Henry came back, and he stiffly walked upstairs to their room. I spoke to Jennie about the many things that gave life meaning, in any position, even in suffering and death. Jennie sighed—her head tipped back, listening to my words. I said she must not struggle against hope, that we must not become miserable or disappointed, no matter the circumstances, because the sun still shone upon the wreckage and the water, and upon everyone and everywhere in the world.

~

APRIL WIND RATTLED THE windows at night as I washed the dishes with Jennie, standing side by side, a light overhead. A misty screen across the moon. Jennie and I were close enough that I'd seen how the lines on her hips had changed from giving birth, as if the waves had shaped her like sand.

Jennie was handing me a plate when I told her about Huran. "Maybe I should've been more like you," I said. "You brought me closer to my son."

"I know what it's like to carry yourself on your shoulders." She teased me, "You're no pushover, ma'am."

We laughed easily. "I'm not talking about me, I'm different, you know."

Jennie splashed me with her fingers.

As it happened in kitchens, I was lulled into staring at nothing at all, and I missed the plate that rolled off the drying rack and crashed onto the floor. In a moment of suspension, I saw the plate as a sphere of light, falling before my eyes, as the very force in my life which had brought me here.

Jennie picked up the silver pieces, tossed them in the trash. "You're lucky that broke just perfectly," and Jennie cleaned and wiped the area by our feet. "Are you okay?"

When I looked at the dry cracks in my heels, I couldn't recognize my feet as my own. They must've been the age of my mother's feet. I nodded at Jennie, and reminded myself how I had rehearsed for this moment: "I think I'm ready to be a mom," I said to her.

"Good," she said. "I'm pretty tired."

This time I flicked the water. "You're not done yet," I said. "The heart of a mother has to fold many times."

"Call me origami," she said, grinning.

"No—jongijeobgi."

Jennie threw her head back. "Yes, exactly!"

"By the way," I said in a serious tone, looking at her. "What's it like, sleeping with my son?"

"I don't know," and she raised an eyebrow at me. "It's kind of like going for a swim." We burst into giggles.

After we dried our hands, I took my mother's green hanbok out from the bundle in my closet.

That night in the living room I dressed Jennie—turning and turning her for the ties. Huran had knotted them tight on me, so I kept them loose. "I never knew the beauty of this hanbok," I said, stepping back, "until I saw it on you."

I called everyone to the living room. Sungho and Henry were refitting the spare room as Haru's new room, putting in skylights. Haru was rolling herself sandals out of jute rope.

"Are you sure?" Jennie exhaled, and her shoulders dropped. "Areumdaweo-yo."

"It's yours," I said. "It was the whole time."

Haru ran down the stairs and into her mother's arms. She squealed to see the hanbok, followed by Sungho and Henry beaming at Jennie, who twirled for them. The lush topmost layer of her skirt glowed. Jennie, buoyed by her glossy reflection, stepped into the foreground, and stood under the chandelier's springing, beaded lights. I stared at her in awe—we all did, even Huran could see how the jacket and full skirt touched Jennie as lovingly as they had me and my mother years ago. The fabric folded smoothly across Jennie's top and draped evenly around her to the floor—the ribbon falling down the front, a new verdant path.

Acknowledgments

IN SOME WAYS, I began the acknowledgments before the book. There was an awareness I tucked away that not only this book but I myself could not have existed without the lives of those who have worked toward reparation and loving perception. My first reader, Elliott Stevens, held these pages for what could burst forth from their fragile shell. Kate McKean gently nudged open the stories following my memoir. Masie Cochran embraced, through lightness and darkness, the many lives of this book. Thank you to Win McCormack, Craig Popelars, Nanci McCloskey, Becky Kraemer, Beth Steidle, and everyone at Tin House. I owe this book to the writers, artists, and scholars who dare to look at history bald in the face: Don Mee Choi, Shawn Wong, Paul Lisicky, Krys Lee, Rowan Hisayo Buchanan, Matthew Salesses, Tayari Jones, Marci Calabretta Cancio-Bello, Crystal Hana Kim, Emily Jungmin Yoon, David Krolikoski, Joseph Han, Greg November, Ed Park, Jimin Han, Jang Wook Huh, Esther Ra, Elizabeth Rosner, and so many others who embody the ideal that bell hooks has expressed: "Without love, our efforts to liberate ourselves and our world community from oppression and exploitation are doomed." I'm grateful to those who make books possible. Things called words and what these things can do are proof of magic. Every morning, before I open my eyes, I hear Adam's and Lily's footsteps—Ari's moonsteps, and *I can wait for you forever*. My deepest hope is to understand that even if we fail, we cannot fail so big as war, and as sure as the sun rises and the world rotates, we as humans have a chance to try again.

Reader's Guide

1. "By an early age, I could read and write in six languages. I found a tool—an ink brush, a twig, or my stub finger—and used it to draw a character on parchment, dirt, or air" (p. 3). How does language carry on through E. J. Koh's *The Liberators*—through different languages but also through poetry and translation and fiction? What is the language of the characters and the language of the story?

2. "I classed *rock, plant, animal, man,* and *God.* I observed a patch of weeds and then myself in the mirror to see the differences between *plant* and *man.* Between them was a middle point, or *animal.* I asked what stood between *man* and *God*" (p. 4). In what ways do hierarchies impact the relationship between ourselves and the world? In what ways do hierarchies oppress relationships between nations and within society and among familial ties?

3. "I realized the wall was never there to begin with. There was never a wall" (p. 128). One of the themes of *The Liberators* is "*borders—real and imaginary.*" In what ways are the relationships between characters affected by borders? In what ways do borders recede, and in what ways do they persist?

4. "It's a little like killing chickens" (p. 59). What are the forces that bring Insuk and Huran together—and what are the forces that drive them apart? What are the similarities and dissimilarities in their beliefs about motherhood—and how are these women tyrannized from within and without?

5. *The Liberators* often brings up historical and intergenerational trauma and a legacy of colonialization and national division—how are different countries connected by their pasts? Where do recurrent traumas appear in each subsequent generation? What events in global history come to mind for you?

6. Sungho differentiates personal memory and state memory through community grieving and public memorials. How does memory change over time, and in what ways can it be affected by personal and state memory? For the Gwangju Massacre, the *Ukishima Maru*, and the *Sewol Ferry* accident, what are the testimonies of the guards and the prisoners, the perpetrators and liberators?

7. "Toto was now in the fields with the mice and the hawks and the rabbits and the foxes and the insects and the fruits and the sun" (p. 83). Animal companionship shapes Henry throughout his life. In what ways do you think animals have shaped the characters and the story—whether it be Toto or the doves or the boar—what do they teach us?

8. "You know why the TV was invented? . . . So presidents can apologize in person. The high resolution is so we can see their tears" (p. 90). What is the role of apology in the lineage of destruction and reparation? What kinds of public and private apologies have you witnessed in the past? How do apologies impede or exacerbate conflict between people and nations?

9. Compare the lineage of the characters—the similarities and differences between parents and children and grandchildren. What beliefs do they share and where do they disagree? How do these beliefs affect what choices the characters make for their future?

10. "We can liberate others because we've already liberated ourselves" (p. 124). How do you define liberation? What are examples of liberation throughout the novel? In what ways do each of the characters liberate each other? In what ways do they liberate themselves?

11. How does lightness coexist with violence in different places and moments in the novel—whether during the protests, or in the prison, or in the townhome, or at the church, or on the ship? How do these places and moments hold disparate ideas and moods and images?

12. The peripheral characters unveil surprising perspectives throughout the novel—the guard, the coroner, Toto, and Tomoko. How do their perspectives contribute to the story and your reading of the novel? How do their testimonies ground us or separate us from reality or the imaginary? What roles do reality and imagination play in the novel?

13. "All those years, I must have believed Sungho was cruel, but when left alone, his joy was larger than my body" (p. 157). How does Insuk and Sungho's relationship change over the course of their courtship and marriage? What do they realize about themselves and their relationship to each other?

14. "Koreans love *Titanic*. Because it's so Korean" (p. 144). What does it mean to be Korean for each of the characters? How do the meanings change over time and for each generation and geography? What differences or similarities do the meanings share—and what do they reveal about the relationship between selfhood and nationhood?

15. "Our problems since the border went up are growing. You know it, without me telling you tonight. The era we live in now deepens inequalities within and between nations. The consequences are landing on ordinary people and causing further divisions in wealth and policies as we grapple with discrimination, tribal nationalism, and greed" (p. 189). What do Robert's words imply about humanity in the face of global inequality and violence? How do other characters agree or disagree with Robert's sense of moral obligation to the Korean peninsula? What are the opposing ideas on the matter of reunification—and what is their significance to the story?

16. Discuss the significance of the titles to each of the parts of the novel: "Invisible Lines," "Animal Kingdom," "Colony of Light," and "The Endling." In what ways do the titles seemingly fit the parts of the novel—and in what ways do they add to your interpretation of the novel?

17. "I said she must not struggle against hope, that we must not become miserable or disappointed, no matter the circumstances, because the sun still shone upon the wreckage and the water, and upon everyone and everywhere in the world" (p. 214). Despite the ongoing circumstances of personal and national tragedy, what does Insuk offer in her words? What does the novel's conclusion suggest about a path toward the future?